Oresund Bridge

Jeannine Dahlberg

authorHOUSE®

AuthorHouse™
1663 Liberty Drive
Bloomington, IN 47403
www.authorhouse.com
Phone: 1-800-839-8640

First published by AuthorHouse 3/4/2010

ISBN: 978-1-4490-7742-6 (e)
ISBN: 978-1-4490-7741-9 (sc)

Library of Congress Control Number: 2010901546

Printed in the United States of America
Bloomington, Indiana

This book is printed on acid-free paper.

FOR

My daughters, grandchildren, brother and niece
*who can be proud of their heritage of a noble legacy
nurtured from a strong foundation of family values.*

AND FOR

My father, grandfather, great grandfather,
and great great grandfather who never will be forgotten.

Other books by Jeannine Dahlberg

****

Featuring Seth Coleman and Rachel Ramsey Coleman

Riding the Tail of the Dragon

Candle in the Window

also

A murder mystery

Evil Web of Deceit

Prologue
(Circa 1958)

Rachel Ramsey Coleman sat all alone in her large, beautifully decorated dark bedroom with only the moon casting a silver thread of light on the balcony. She was mentally depressed with sullen thoughts, which had no conjectural answers; and she could not control this pensive mood swing, which was more prevalent around ten o'clock at night when she and Seth Coleman would think of one another regardless of where they were in the world. She looks longingly at the large king-size bed and remembers their lover's nightly ritual of holding hands while falling asleep. Her heart aches for Seth's touch.

Fluffy pillows on the over-size lounge chair provided some comfort as tears streamed down her cheeks. She wiped her eyes in disbelief and stepped outside onto the balcony. With blurred, wet eyes she slowly scanned the manicured lawn to the calm water of the largest lake on her newly inherited plantation in Virginia, as if looking for answers to her many perplexing questions. She stood quietly... with her eyes transfixed on a few white water lilies blooming at the edge of the lake where Seth proposed marriage three years ago. With a rush of emotions, she relived the memory of that evening and the pernicious events that brought them together as man and wife. It was a whirlwind courtship, which spanned two continents.

A falling star distracted Rachel for a few moments from her hypnotic trance of thoughts as she stood on the moonlit balcony. She quickly made a wish, which turned more into a prayer... hoping Seth is thinking about her at this hour... and she continued to weep. In a dream-like state, she slowly closed her eyes and created a visual image of the first time she saw Seth. He was standing at the railing of the tramp steamer *Ladybug* looking at the beautiful view of Hong Kong while the ship was anchored in Victoria Harbor. She had moored her small sampan along side the ship to pick up a passenger destined for the island of Lantau. She will never forget how handsome he looked as he peered down at her with eyes filled with curiosity. She imagined he was thinking: *what is a Caucasian woman with blonde hair doing on a small sampan in Victoria Harbor.* It was only a few days later she learned he had come to China to search for her.

Rachel blinked away the tears from her eyes and with a brief feeling of happiness recalled how enthusiastic Seth became when he talked about her returning to the States to inherit one of the largest tobacco plantations in Virginia. They spent hours together while Seth proceeded to tell her the story of her birth and adoption as was told to him by Inspector Claude LeCleur of the Interpol office in Paris... a story, which was beyond her comprehension that she was the sole heir of a plantation... a story, which was a revelation of her adoption... a story that she had *never* heard. It was a poignant story, which was extremely distressing for Rachel to hear and learn of her birth and adoption from a total stranger.

———

Rachel's mother, Alice Ramsey, fled the Ramsey plantation to escape from a miserable marriage. She wanted to build a new life in Paris, leaving her old life and everyone she knew behind her. To her dismay, she was pregnant and she died giving birth to Rachel in Paris, France shortly before World War II. Baby Rachel was immediately placed in the Orleans Orphanage; and months later, she was adopted by General Erik von Horstmann and his wife.

During the war years, the general carved an impressive military career while serving with Hitler's Third Reich army in North Africa with Field Marshal Rommel and the 7th Panzer Division. It was after the second battle of el-Alamein when Rommel's Panzers were defeated that Hitler ordered General von Horstmann and General Rommel to return to Western Europe to set up German defenses fortifying the Atlantic Wall along the occupied French coast. Hitler believed it was inevitable that the Western Allies would invade Europe through France or Belgium; and on June 6, 1944, Allied forces successfully invaded Normandy… physically crushing the German military forces and the prideful spirit of the German officers.

After the costly defeat of the German army at Stalingrad on the Eastern Front, many high-ranking officers believed it was only a matter of time before Nazi Germany would surrender. To prevent this from happening, they wanted to eliminate Hitler and open negotiations with the Allies for honorable peace terms. There were many plots to assassinate Hitler… and Rachel's father was involved with one that was given the code name Operation Valkyrie. But by this time, Hitler was well aware of the assassination attempts and made his movements as unpredictable as possible. Operation Valkyrie failed horribly. Many high-ranking officers were killed by Hitler's SS troops and many took their own life, including Field Marshall Rommel.

Taking extreme precautions, General von Horstmann managed to get Frau Horstmann and Rachel out of Berlin and escape to Paris where they sought asylum with the French underground. When confronted by Inspector LeCleur and officers of the French Resistance, General von Horstmann explained he was privy to top-secret knowledge of the assassination plot to kill Churchill. In return for divulging the vital information required to thwart the attack, he demanded safe passage for him and his family to the neutral island of Macau, which is a short distance from Hong Kong, China up the Pearl River Estuary. Of course, the French Resistance eagerly accepted his demand.

The family had established residence in Macau for only a few months when General von Horstmann was approached by British Intelligence and French Interpol to head the intelligence office in the orient on the island of Lantau. With his extensive military experience, and a letter of recommendation from Inspector LeCleur, he was the perfect candidate to work closely with the foreign offices in an effort to quell the rapid expansion of drug trafficking and gold smuggling in Hong Kong and Macau. The general eagerly accepted the position to have the opportunity once again to strategically plan against an enemy. And, this time, the enemy was the Triad Society of Hong Kong.

Rachel remembered how quietly she sat trying to absorb the biographical record of her adoption while Seth told the story with alacrity and compassion bringing details of Rachel's early life to a time when her own memories were sparked into awareness of her youth; and her thoughts continued to ramble.

She remembered it was her mother who devised the plan to build an orphanage on Lantau, which would be cover for the general's headquarters and military compound. The orphanage would also accommodate all the children who came out of the hills seeking refuge from the war.

A warmth of tenderness rippled through her body as she recalled her teen years growing up in the military compound where the welfare of the children in the orphanage became her priority. She spent hours teaching and telling stories, which helped to bring happiness into their lives. The children loved her for their new feeling of security and compassion... emotions they had never experienced. She remembered how she and her mother listened to her dad discuss the many problems incurred in his new position on Lantau. It was in China where the family became a tight threesome, when out of necessity they learned to depend on one another in a new foreign country.

The coolness of the night air made Rachel shiver, but for the moment, she was happy to remain on the balcony to recall memories of her youth. She continued her thoughts hoping they would help her decide if she really wants to return to the orphanage on Lantau or remain on the plantation. She wiped the tears from her eyes and with a slight smile on her lips recalled how energetic Seth became when he vividly described the plantation.

———

Seth literally beamed with pride when he spoke of his family, the Colemans, being the managers of the plantation for many generations. It was his father, BillyJoe, who asked him to find Rachel so she could claim ownership of the property and remove it from the probate courts.

Seth reported with passion that he knew every facet of the operation of the plantation and explained that as a teenager he was a tour guide during the summer months. He fervently described the restored antebellum Ramsey mansion as being one of the most beautiful in the tidewater region of Virginia. The plantation was a "must see" of mansions and plantations in the South... topping the tour list. He explained tourists are still fascinated with the stories told of the aristocratic Ramsey family and their opulent lifestyle, which many years ago included extravagant balls, exciting hunting parties and visits by European royalty.

He elaborated upon the six thousand acres of rich farmland, which yield copious crops of tobacco, while the many lakes afford a picturesque, pristine beauty. He further stated: after the Great Depression, the Ramseys expanded their interest from growing tobacco to include diversifying in the banking industry and commodities market. Consequently, for many generations the Ramsey name has been synonymous with money and power.

Rachel leaned against the balcony railing unable to control the tears. The moon was on the wane, now, casting only a slight glimmer of light as the night hours ticked away. Loneliness swelled in her heart creating a heavy, sick feeling taking her into the depth of despair. She looked upward into the depth of heaven pleading for help to restore their marriage and   obliterate the memory of the miserable turn of events, which prompted a bitter argument.

Part I

Chapter One

The plane cruised at twenty-seven thousand feet in a bright star-studded sky bound for Stockholm, Sweden. It was ten o'clock at night and Seth was immersed in thoughts of Rachel. He languished in a state of depression thinking of the regrettable argument they had before he left to catch the plane. It was their first big argument since they married. They had their share of a few minor disagreements, but nothing of this volatile magnitude. He reprimanded himself for storming out of the house without kissing Rachel; and he could not believe he actually said *good-bye*. He hated the word as it has a sound of finality. He preferred to say "so long" or "see ya". His mental disposition teetered from self-reproach of words vehemently spoken to being steadfast in his concern for Rachel's safety if she returns to China.

A bumpy landing on the tarmac startled Seth to bleak reality as the plane slowly maneuvered to the terminal in Stockholm. It was seven-thirty in the morning and his friend Nils was going to meet him at the arrival gate. He packed only one carry-on, which he jammed into the overhead compartment above his seat thereby avoiding delay at the luggage carousel.

With a fast stride in his step up the long ramp, Seth was eager to depart the plane to see his friend again. It had been quite awhile since they lived together on campus at Washington University in St. Louis, Missouri, where they both studied design and architecture.

"Seth! Hey buddy, over here," a voice called from the confused melee of people in the terminal.

With a big grin, Seth called, "I was looking for your curly blonde hair, but I think everyone here has blonde hair. How are you doing, curly top?"

"Yeah! Well, you know, we Vikings are all blonde; and let's drop the curly top. College days are in the past." Nils jokingly informed and queried, "Where is your wife? I thought she was coming, too."

"Don't ask," Seth doggedly replied. "It's a long story."

The two friends scurried to the parking lot where Nils had parked his Volvo. The drive from the airport to the SAS Royal Viking Hotel in Stockholm was enjoyable for both men as they laughed and bantered back and forth the life-style and shenanigans of living in a fraternity house. The tone of conversation turned more serious, however, when they started to discuss the purpose for Seth's visit to Sweden.

Nils reported, "The architectural students at Lund University are looking forward to your lecture on urban sprawl, town planning and land use." He slowly shook his head from side-to-side and asked, "What I want to know, Seth, is: how did you get all that nice publicity for your design of the town houses in the south-side Chicago area? Was 'lady luck' riding with you?" Nils continued, "The article you wrote for the *International Architectural Institute* magazine jump-started your career quickly and you have already carved quite a nice reputation among your peers."

"I guess you could say 'lady luck' was with me, but I like to think the positive forces of feng shui are with me." Seth quickly answered.

With a silly smirk on his face, Nils questioned in a condescending tone, "Okay. What is feng shui?"

"I have learned a lot about the Chinese philosophy of feng shui since I traveled to China; and my wife, Rachel, is a diehard believer in the ancient art and science of balancing the earth's energies for health and good fortune." Seth stopped to ponder his thought, but then just quietly mentioned, "That is another long story... with a simple answer to a complex question.

"Nils, I think it's great you are taking a few days vacation to spend time with me while I am in Sweden. I want to see a little bit of this beautiful country before attending to business in Lund."

The two sat quietly for a short time while Nils drove through the streets of Stockholm to the hotel, which was conveniently located a couple blocks from the train station. He was careful not to drive the heavily traveled ones taken by tourists, as the hour for the changing of the guard at the City Palace was fast approaching. Seth assumed it was the height of the tourist season and the crowds of people hustling to the train station and bus terminal easily confirmed his thought.

After checking into the hotel, the two young men spent the afternoon leisurely wandering through the walking streets of the city central district enjoying the sights and sounds. Musicians and magicians entertained at most street corners and vendors offered Scandinavian-made items for sale to entice the tourists.

A little nip in the air contributed to a pleasant boat excursion of Lake Malaren and Nils was the perfect tour guide. He explained in a pundit style: "Stockholm is called the Venice of the North, as it is comprised of fourteen islands surrounded by Lake Malaren and the Baltic Sea. You can get a great view of our beautiful City Hall, which is there on your right; and I guess you know it is famous for hosting the Nobel Peace Prize awards in the spacious Blue Hall, which seats thirteen hundred people."

The boat continued a slow journey, passing several nude beaches along the way to its destination Drottningholm Palace, which is the summer residence of the king and queen. Tourists were not allowed inside, but the beautiful landscape, which was fashioned after the gardens at the Palace of Versailles in Paris, was well worth the trip. Both men, being architects, also enjoyed the structural design of the palace and studied it from every angle.

It was early evening when the boat returned to the dock and Seth was beginning to feel the affects of lack of sleep from the long plane flight.

With a gaping yawn, Seth suggested, "What do you say we go back to the hotel for a cocktail and an early dinner?"

"Sounds good to me." Nils was fast to reply and jokingly posed a question, "How did you like having your own private tour guide?"

3

and explained, "When I was in high school, I worked for one of the largest tour companies in Stockholm during the summer and saved enough money to go to college in the United States. Of course, it helped that my dad owns the company."

"Well, if I were grading you on the curve, I would have to give you an 'I' for inferior," Seth sarcastically teased.

"What?" Nils blurted.

"Well, Nils, you forgot to bring the binoculars so I could see the bathers on the nude beaches!"

Both men laughed and agreed the trip would have been even more interesting with binoculars.

———

The two sat in the hotel dining room quietly relaxing while sipping an Absolute vodka martini, which restored their energy level and got them talking again. They continued to reminisce about college days when the waiter presented the menu. Seth carefully read the entrees, which were predominately fish, and decided to try the Swedish meatballs.

Nils started to laugh at his choice. "You would not make a good Swede if you don't like fish." Nils suggested with a wink of his eye at the waiter, "Why don't you try lutefisk? You may like it;" and nonchalantly posed, "It's just dried codfish."

Seth grimaced with an expression of horror on his face, "Yeah, sure. Are you trying to kill me? Even in the States, lutefisk does not appeal to the civilized taste buds for an acquired delicacy. Maybe the Vikings liked it, but good grief, man! It's soaked in a water-lye solution before cooking and has a wickedly caustic taste."

"Well, why don't you order from the smorgasbord table where there is a larger selection of food. After all, you're in Sweden." Nils continued to laugh at Seth's frustration.

"No thanks, I'll stick with the meatballs," and Seth handed the menu to the waiter.

The two lingered awhile longer at the table over dinner discussing plans for the next few days. "I have made hotel reservations for us in Malmo for two days before we travel to Lund University for my lecture." Seth advised.

"What's in Malmo that you want to see?" Nils asked.

"Do you remember Fritz Dahl at Wash U? After we graduated, we were both drafted into the army and, coincidently, we served in the same army unit in Korea." Seth bowed his head trying to shake off the thought of war and continued, "Fritz and I became very close and more or less looked after one another. We stayed in touch after we were mustered out of service and kept track of our professional accomplishments... and he called me before I left home."

Seth sat quietly for awhile, sipping the martini, and trying to forget his life as a forward observer during the war. Nils knew he was remembering something about the war that he has been trying to forget and did not interrupt his solitude.

Finally, Seth continued, "If you remember, Fritz studied civil engineering and structural design. Well, he is quite interested in a project that is on the table for Sweden and Denmark to connect the metropolitan areas of Malmo, Sweden and Copenhagen, Denmark... a distance of water spanning over ten miles across the Oresund Strait." Seth reported and doubtfully surmised, "I, personally, think that is a pretty grandiose project and is far off into the future."

"Wow!" Nils responded in wonderment, "It would be exciting to work on a project of that magnitude... one that has never before been accomplished." He continued with his curious thought, "I know France and England considered a similar project for the English Channel in the early 1800s and even Napoleon toyed with the idea of connecting the two countries, but then he became too involved with wars."

Both men sat quietly... embroiled in their own confused thoughts of *how can such a masterpiece of design be accomplished?* Both rationalized: *Only time will tell.*

With a brighter thought Seth added, "But if you remember, Fritz graduated with top honors in our class and I bet he is involved with the project design. Fritz said he read my article in the magazine and wanted to talk to me when I arrived in Sweden." Seth paused to ask the question, "Nils, do you remember when the three of us were locked out of the fraternity house and spent the night on the lawn talking about everything and anything."

"Yeah! How could I forget that prank our frat brothers played on us." Nils was fast to reply.

Seth urged, "Nils I know you must remember when Fritz told us his ancestors are Swedish... and then you two started talking in Swedish. I think you were talking about me, because you two were sure laughing while looking at me and didn't give me a clue as to what was being said."

Nils jokingly punched Seth on the arm, "You're absolutely right! We were laughing at you... hell man, we had a great time that night. I'll never forget it."

Seth let it pass he will never know what was so funny and called to the waiter for another vodka martini.

"As I recall," Seth ventured to tell the story, "Fritz was born in Malmo and is the great, great grandson of Carl Edward Vilhem (Edward Count Piper of Sweden). In order to place that into a time-frame for us," Seth continued, "he said Edward Count Piper was the minister resident, or ambassador, from Sweden and Norway to the United States at the time of Abraham Lincoln's presidency and they became good friends."

Nils was wondering why this was an important story for the two of them to remember, but remained silent as Seth continued.

"The castle, Christinehof Slot, which was the family home, is now a tourist attraction, and is east of Malmo close to the Baltic Sea. Fritz asked me to take the morning tour bus there to meet him and asked that I pretend to be a tourist. He said he had some important information he wanted to share with me before I go to Lund University. He made it sound mysterious; and it was definitely an urgent request."

Nils interrupted and reminded Seth, "What in the world is that all about, but if you remember Fritz always had a flair for the dramatic."

Seth was dumbfounded with the request, also, but stated, "I told him you were traveling with me to Lund and he said, 'Great! Bring Nils, too.'"

They both sat quietly at the table, sipping their martini, trying to figure out what was so important that would necessitate they immediately travel to Christinehof to meet Fritz. They pondered the thought for a short while; but with no viable answer to the perplexing question, they decided to turn in for the night.

Chapter Two

Early the next morning, Seth and Nils met in the lobby for a continental breakfast and then hustled by foot to the train station to catch the express train to Malmo, which is a considerable distance southwest from Stockholm.

Nils regretted Seth's short visit to his beautiful city. His experience as a tour guide afforded extensive knowledge of the surrounding area and he had hoped to show Seth more tourist attractions; such as, the House of Royalty, the Vasa Museum, the old city square with the fourteenth century water fountain, the changing of the guard at the City Palace, the opera house, and the turbulent water of Lake Malaren where it flows into the Baltic Sea. For two- of the five-hour train ride to Malmo, Nils expanded on the glorious sites and the significant influence the Vikings had over many countries for several centuries in the historical past.

Seth tried to be attentive to the long, interesting commentary, but his fretful thoughts popped into his mind as flash backs to the afternoon he left Rachel standing in the foyer of the Ramsey mansion. She was crying, but he thought she looked beautiful and he dwelled upon that vision. He felt his heart swell with love and longed to kiss her. He slumped in his seat dejected with a feeling of tenderness and persistently yearned to hold her in his arms.

His thoughts were but a short interlude to realizing he must place a call to his dad, BillyJoe, who is now co-owner of the plantation, to ask if Rachel has returned to Lantau, China, to visit her father and to assist with running the children's orphanage. She explained to Seth because of the economic unrest, a great number of children are once again starting to come to the orphanage to live.

Seth's concern is for her safety at a time when mainland China, under the communist leadership of Chairman Mao Tse-tung, is making an ambitious attempt to modernize the Chinese economy in a Great Leap Forward program and China is feeling pains from communist control.

The peasants and university students in Beijing are becoming restless and Seth has read there may be a cultural revolution.

In the short span of time Rachel and Seth have known one another, they have survived many trials and tribulations: including surviving World War II in Europe, kidnapping, a tsunami, confrontations with the notorious Chinese Triad smugglers in Hong Kong, Seth's military service in the Korean War… and Seth is overwhelmed and thankful their love has sustained them through these difficult life-threatening situations. He looks out the train window to the heaven above with a prayerful thought of "thanks" and closes his eyes. He regrets he will have to wait until tonight to place the call to his dad.

Yet another perplexing thought popped into his mind: Fritz's urgent request to meet him at Christinehof. Seth opened his eyes to stare out the train window… looking, but not seeing the beautiful countryside in an array of green forest land and crystal blue lakes.

It was mid-afternoon when the train pulled into the station in Malmo. Seth awoke Nils, who had nodded off to sleep, and the two walked quickly to the Radisson Hotel, which was located only a few blocks away.

———

The hotel room was quite comfortable with two queen-size beds and Seth grabbed the phone right away to place a call to Fritz. "Hi, we just arrived," Seth reported.

"The train made good time. I didn't expect your call so soon. Is Nils with you?" Fritz asked.

"Yeah, he slept a couple of hours on the train and he is already lying on the bed with his eyes closed." Seth continued, "Well, we had a late night and I think too many Absolute vodka martinis."

"Seth," Fritz quietly murmured, "I want you to make tour reservations for tomorrow morning with the concierge in the hotel lobby to come to Christinehof. The tour will leave your hotel at ten o'clock and you should get here by eleven. I will be working in the gift shop and will not be able to talk to you at that time, but I want you to buy a rather large duffel bag, which I will show you and something for your wife. And please do not indicate in any way that you know me… and tell Nils not to show that he knows me." Fritz continued in a very quiet voice, as if he did not want anyone to hear him, "The tour group will stay for lunch at Christinehof and I will introduce myself to the tour group and will join you for lunch. Do you understand?"

Seth was quick to reply, "Not really! I will ask my questions tomorrow."

"Okay, see you tomorrow."

Seth heard the receiver click and spun around to talk to Nils.

"That was another interesting conversation." Seth lamented. "Fritz must be involved in something that may be dangerous and I guess we will have to wait until tomorrow to find out what it is." Seth looked at Nils with eyes wide in a look of confusion and volunteered, "Fritz sure can be melodramatic.

"Come on, Nils, get up!" Seth urged. "We have to get our tour tickets for tomorrow."

The two young men were surprised to see the hotel lobby filled with people waiting to be escorted on various tours standing by a rather large poster at the information desk advertising the Malmo Festival, which was scheduled for the next three days. The city was prepared to welcome people from many European countries who would participate in many activities. The poster advertised a canoe race on the canal around the old town; band concerts in Folketspark; folk dancers performing traditional dances on street corners; and exotic food.

They pushed their way through the crowd to the concierge's desk to purchase tickets for the morning tour to Christinehof and were happy there were still a few seats available.

Seth proclaimed, "Let's play like a tourist and walk the streets of Malmo. We may as well enjoy ourselves, now. Who knows what tomorrow will bring."

Chapter Three

The morning sun came up and blessed the sky in a power of brightness that filtered through the hotel window awaking Seth. His first thought was: *how can it be a beautiful morning when I am in the depth of despair.* The late night phone call to his dad did not yield the information he wanted to hear. His dad's message reverberated in his head like an echo bouncing in sound waves from one mountain to another. Over and over again he could hear BillyJoe say, "Rachel left this morning for Hong Kong."

Seth sat up in bed in a cold sweat remembering his last dreadful conversation with Rachel when she declared: "My decision to return to China has not been an easy one. I have given much thought to the point I believed my brain was going to burst... but I must follow my heart. There are adverse fields of energy on this plantation, which are detrimental in health and well-being to the women who have lived in this house." Seth could hear the tone of her voice condescend with the thought, "You must know this to be true from stories told to you about your mother, and my mother, and Miss Patty, and other women before her."

Seth vigorously punched his pillow with his fist causing the springs in his bed to rattle, which noise awoke Nils.

"Hey, man!" Nils emphatically blurted, "I hope I wasn't in that dream!"

With blank stares, the two just looked at one another for a few seconds, but Seth did not volunteer an explanation and Nils fell back to sleep.

"Come on, Nils! Get up! I want to grab a bite to eat before we have to board the tour bus." Seth called.

The marvelous aroma from hot coffee brewing came from the dining room, which was crowded with eager tourists wanting to enjoy a good breakfast... and the large selection of fruit, various cuts of cheese, bread, sweet rolls, pancakes, sausage, cold cuts, coffee, juice and more at the smorgasbord table more than satisfied their appetite. Everyone was ready to start the trip.

The bus was filled to capacity and most tourists enjoyed the countryside drive through the rolling hills to the Baltic Sea while some slept. The tour guide was thorough in his commentary, stating: "Southeast Sweden is known as the breadbasket of the country, as the many fields of crops supply most of the food for Sweden's cities and northern mountain populated areas. Christinehof castle estate has an estimated thirteen thousand hectares rich in forest land where an abundance of wild life roams. Christina owned several other estates, which together totaled over twenty thousand hectares or most of Skane Province." The tour guide paused and then continued to explain: "Until a short time ago, it was the game keeper (or squire) whose responsibility was to hunt the animals to furnish meat for the table."

Seth leaned over to Nils and whispered, "I remember Fritz telling us that night on the lawn at the frat house, that it was his great grandfather who was the game keeper for Christinehof." Nils nodded in agreement.

The bus traveled over a few creeks that flow with a red color of alum sulfate, which is a mined product used for many chemical processes; and the tour guide clarified the tourists' curiosity for the red/brown color of the water. "Christina Piper purchased the property and built the castle in the mid 1700s. The property included a failing business of mining alum; and being a highly intelligent woman, she turned the business into a successful operation. At one time, it employed hundreds of people; had its own school, fire station and even printed its own money. The alum industry is no longer in existence, but a charming village, which is now uninhabited, remains."

The bus continued to rumble along the narrow road and the tour guide mentioned, "During the summertime, popular musicians from around the world perform concerts on the estate, drawing huge crowds of fans from all over Europe." He paused in his commentary as the castle came into view and informed the group that the castle has been converted into a museum, but it does have a few guest rooms.

Christinehof castle held a formidable position at the end of the long driveway, with a rather large building on each side… one housed the old horse-drawn carriages of previous years; and the other building has been renovated to accommodate a restaurant. Seth presumed this is where the tour group will have lunch.

The two architects immediately noticed the construction of Christinehof is not the typical German-style castle. The design is German baroque with a mansard roof and the façade of the castle is painted a yellow ochre color of unparalleled intensity. With a look of surprise, Seth and Nils continued to study the design.

The tour bus pulled to a stop at a distance from the buildings and the tour guide suggested the immediate surroundings of the castle would be seen first before going inside the castle. It was a long walking tour of the property, which Seth and Nils found to be interesting, but they were eager to see Fritz in the gift shop. Finally, after viewing a number of rooms in the castle, which have been maintained in the same décor as in Christina's day, the tourists were taken to the gift shop for browsing before a late lunch.

Seth and Nils noticed there were a few more tour busses parked in the lot, which explained the crowd of tourists mulling around the common area between the gift shop and restaurant. The two slowly pushed their way through the entrance and easily recognized Fritz, as he is quite tall, standing behind a display case assisting shoppers. He gave Seth and Nils a high-sign of recognition with his eyes as the two circled the gift shop looking at various items of interest. They paused at the display cases of Kosta lead crystal glass and admired the superior, artistic workmanship of one of the vases.

Fritz approached the two, and in a helpful salesmanship manner asked, "May I show you something from the case?"

Seth quickly responded, "Yes, I am interested in buying a vase for my wife and I also would like to purchase a duffel bag for me. I noticed as I entered the shop that you have several on display."

Fritz removed the vase from the case and directed the two toward the front of the shop. There was a nice selection of duffel bags in various sizes and Seth chose a small one.

"If you like a larger size bag, you could carry your crystal vase inside, protecting it from breaking and you could probably carry it with you on the plane." Fritz urged.

"I think that is a good idea!" Seth replied. "I prefer the dark blue heavy woolen duffel bag with the Swedish crown in gold embroidered on the side."

"Good choice. I'll take the vase in the back, wrap it securely in bubble wrap and put it in your duffel bag." Fritz vanished through a private door to the back of the shop. When he returned, he handed the bag to Seth, along with the sales receipt, and mentioned that he put an additional copy of the sales receipt inside the bag for custom purposes, suggesting Seth read it for accuracy when he returns to the hotel.

Seth thought: *That doesn't make any sense. If it is a copy of the receipt he just handed me so I can purchase the items at the cashier's station, the receipt in the bag should be identical. I guess he wants me to be sure to read something on the receipt.*

Fritz interrupted Seth's thought: "I think your tour guide is motioning for his group of tourists to go to the restaurant for lunch," and directed his question to the tour guide, "I haven't had lunch, yet, and I would like to join your group, if it is okay?"

The tour guide was quick to respond. "Sure, come along."

The restaurant was quite large and beautifully decorated in typical Scandinavian fashion with many different size tables. The tour guide suggested Fritz join him at a table for four and Seth and Nils were quick to sit down, also.

The conversation at the table was rather mundane for Seth and Nils while the tour guide and Fritz discussed the prosperous tourist season. Fritz mentioned he recognized one couple had recently visited twice before and asked if the tour guide knew the couple's purpose in visiting the castle three times.

Nils and Seth turned to look at the couple who were seated near the entrance. It appeared they were not talking and were concentrating on the food on their plate... almost hovering over the table with their shoulders lowered in a peculiar manner. The man wore a black sweatshirt with Stockholm in yellow letters on the front and the woman wore a blue and yellow hat with Stockholm printed on the brim. They looked like the typical tourists sporting clothes purchased from their last city tour; and Seth remembered seeing them at breakfast and assumes they are registered at the same hotel.

With a shrug of his shoulders and a toss of his head, the tour guide volunteered, "They are a rather strange couple. They never talk... not even to one another. In fact, they both sleep on the bus going and returning; and I never have had a tourist take the same tour three times in a row." The tour guide chuckled and said, "Either I'm an interesting guide or they like to sleep on a bus, or they are really strange."

Fritz asked Nils and Seth, "What do you think?"

All four turned to look at the couple as if digesting what had just been said. Fritz wanted to call Nils' and Seth's attention to the couple again so they could recognize them if they should happen to see them elsewhere.

The tour guide looked at his watch and motioned for his tourist group to board the bus to return to Malmo. With a quick handshake and a smile, Fritz looked at Seth and affirmed, "Enjoy your new duffel bag!"

Seth and Nils were disappointed they did not have an opportunity to be alone with Fritz to ask the many questions about their mysterious visit to Christinehof. Fritz spoke only to the tour guide and was more concerned with the odd couple who had taken the tour three times. Seth could only assume they would find their answers in the duffel bag.

Chapter Four

The odd couple pushed into the line to board the bus directly behind Seth and Nils; and Seth thought it strange the man kept nudging his knee against the duffel bag. Seth became uneasy when they took seats directly across the aisle from them and noticed they paid close attention when the duffel bag was stored above in the storage rack. The atmosphere was quiet with very little conversation among the tourists and most slept on the return trip to Malmo. Seth and Nils looked at one another with eyebrows raised and a curious stare, but said nothing, as they glanced across the aisle at the odd couple who were sleeping. The man emitted a snoring sound on occasion and appeared to be quite comfortable with his legs stretched into the aisle. Seth noticed his good-looking mahogany brown leather boots with a pewter/bronze metallic buckle and made a blind guess the boots were handmade in the mountains of Italy… and had to be very expensive. The boots reminded Seth of his childhood days living on the Ramsey plantation, when on occasion old man Ramsey, the patriarch, wore a similar pair of boots with a shiny buckle, which were made in Italy.

The return trip to Malmo seemed to go faster; and after the tour bus pulled to the front of the hotel, Seth and Nils decided to let everyone get off first. Seth grabbed the duffel bag and protected the contents from the hustling crowd. He definitely did not want the expensive vase to break. The tour guide was already at the hotel door when Seth called to him, "Wait up! Do you have a minute?"

"Of course," and jokingly asked, "Do you want to go on the trip again tomorrow?"

Seth and Nils gave a slight smile and in return Seth asked, "Well, I would like to know if the odd couple has signed to take the tour again tomorrow."

"No, they haven't and I won't miss them," and asked the question, "Are you both staying in Malmo tomorrow?"

Nils was quick to answer, "We are taking the train tomorrow to Lund." With a friendly pat on Seth's back continued, "My buddy, here, is going to give a lecture at Lund University in the afternoon, but we will return to the hotel in Malmo in the evening."

"A lecture at Lund University," the tour guide repeated. "I'm impressed! Visiting professors and students come from all over the world to attend various lectures. It is an international center for education... and it is one of the best. It is internationally recognized for research and commercial activities with many important companies located in the vicinity." The tour guide stopped to catch his breath, smiled and reluctantly admitted, "I sound like a salesman pitching for the university. Maybe, I should give up guiding tours." He kicked his boot in the gravel, bowed his head in respect, and continued, "It's my alma mater and I miss living in Lund where the atmosphere is vibrant and stimulating. I'm beginning to find my job as a tour guide to be boring. I could give the palaver in my sleep."

The three men stood silently for a few minutes... each deep in thought.

Nils thought: *I think this guy missed his calling. He should be on the payroll for Lund University scouting for new students.*

Seth was concerned: *I haven't had a chance to think about my lecture tomorrow. Perhaps, I will have some quiet time tonight to go over my notes.* Seth rationalized: *Well, the article I wrote for the magazine contains most of the information I plan to discuss, anyway.* With a feeling to bolster his confidence: *I think my preparation for this lecture is more than sufficient.* He felt a pang of mental anguish: *I wonder if Rachel is thinking of me?*

The tour guide broke the silence and suggested, "I may try to hear your lecture tomorrow, if I can." With a cheery good-bye, he left the two and returned to the bus.

———

Seth cradled the duffel bag in his arms as both hurried through the hotel lobby to catch an elevator to their room. They were anxious to read what was written on the sales slip. With a quick step, Seth rushed to the table by the window to put the bag under the direct sunlight. His face said it all when he peered into the bag. Nils could easily read his disappointment. "Okay, other than a lot of bubble wrap around a vase, what do we have?"

Seth removed the expensive vase with caution and found a long note from Fritz. Before reading the note, Seth also removed a stack of preliminary plans and schematic drawings tucked inside. With a confused expression of surprise, Nils blindly asked, "What in the world is all this?"

The two sat at the table to examine what they had just found in the duffel bag. They studied the contents for a long time digesting the enormity of the proposed project displayed before them. As Seth had surmised, Fritz was involved to a far greater extent with the proposed project to connect Malmo, Sweden and Copenhagen, Denmark; suggesting a suspension bridge from Malmo to a man-made island; with the project continuing under water by tunnel to Copenhagen. Not all the blueprints for the complete project were enclosed... only those requiring patents. Seth could visualize the time and effort involved in creating this magnificent project.

Both men are well aware of industrial espionage, which frequently exists among companies seeking to gain access to rival company plans or trade secrets. Large companies expect some form of industrial espionage to be practiced against them and will hire security personnel who work specifically to guard against such spying. Very seldom is violence involved; but when the spies are successful in obtaining the valued information, the loss can cost the company millions upon millions of dollars. Now, both men can understand the need for caution in transporting these plans, as patents for certain innovative ideas indicated have not been obtained, as yet. If they should fall into the hands of a competing architectural firm, it would be a disaster for Fritz and his company.

Seth continued to read the long note where Fritz outlined the need for secrecy in delivering the duffel bag with the enclosed contents of plans to Karl Larsson at Lund University. The note went on to explain, "Karl is a mechanical engineer and a good friend of mine from Denmark, who will contact you before your lecture." The note requested, "When he approaches you, ask him what university he attended... and he will answer with the password, Wash U."

The note ended with the caveat: "I'd hate to say guard the duffel bag with your life since you both think I have a flair for the dramatic... but guard it with your life!"

"Hell! What has Fritz gotten us into, now?" Nils erupted spewing the story, "Remember on campus when Fritz accused a fraternity pledge of stealing from his brothers and everyone started sneaking around spying on each other. He really raised a big rigamarole and I didn't think he would ever quit with his accusations."

Seth urged, "Quiet! Keep your voice down. These hotel rooms have thin walls." Seth cautioned, "Yes, I remember. That's been quite a few years ago; and if you remember, Fritz caught the pledge one night sneaking around the house looking for money while we were asleep.

"Hey, Nils, you are speaking better English. You're even using some of our slang words in your vocabulary. Rigamarole?" And they both laughed.

Chapter Five

S leep did not come easily to Seth and Nils. The long night melted into early morning hours before either one fell asleep as both felt the pressure of the activities of the previous day. The irritating buzz of the alarm clock rang too early, which caused their temperament to bristle into a sensitive mood, as they continued to toss and turn in bed a little longer. Seth was the first to get up to shower and shave as he wanted to study his notes for his lecture before Nils got out of bed. When he believed he had gone over all the important points of his lecture, he turned his thoughts to the problem at hand… the duffel bag. He gently removed the expensive vase from the duffel bag and left some of the bubble wrap on top of the architectural drawings and preliminary plans making certain they could not be seen if the bag were opened.

The two scurried to the dining room for a quick breakfast before boarding the train to Lund. Both scanned the crowded room looking for the odd couple, but did not see them. Seth placed the duffel bag next to his feet on the floor and bowed his head to adjust the bag next to his leg so he could feel it at all times. He glanced across the aisle and noticed a shiny buckle on the man's boot. At first, he did not recognize the man and woman sitting at the table, but thought: *what are the odds of someone having the same identical boots. It's a stroke of luck I looked down.* He paid closer attention to the man, who was wearing a tie and sport jacket with his black hair combed straight back from a receding hairline. The woman wore a fashionable white and black boucle jacket with black slacks and no hat. Her auburn hair fell to a shoulder-length cut. The odd couple held their head down while they ate and said nothing.

Seth looked at Nils and gave him a high-sign to look down at the table across the aisle. Both said nothing, ate a fast breakfast; and almost ran to the train station a few blocks away. Seth held tightly to the duffel bag, turning many times to see if they were being followed. The odd couple was not in sight. Both felt their imagination was playing tricks with them and breathed a sigh of relief.

They purchased their tickets to Lund and boarded a beautifully painted train, with the engine in purple with a red stripe and a white bird emblem on the front. The railway passenger car was named after Per Albin Hansson, who was the Prime Minister for the Socialist Democratic Party in Sweden and was elected four times in the 1930s and 40s. Once again Seth recalled his conversation with Fritz during college days when Fritz stated: "My grandfather and Per Albin Hansson were good friends in the early 1900s, when they both worked for the Social Democratic Youth Association to reform social and economic policies established by the King.

Per Albin Hansson was a journalist for the party paper, *Fram* or *Forward*, and later became the editor of the *Social-Demokraten.* My grandfather was a custom officer for the King working in Malmo, and was the Secretary/Treasurer of the party. The Swedish people are very proud of these men… for their dedication in giving the Swedish people a better way of life."

Seth paused in his thought and remembered Fritz said: "When my dad was a young boy, he would sit on Per Albin Hansson's lap when grandfather and Per Albin would play chess. They both really enjoyed the skill of the game."

Lund was less than an hour's distance from Malmo by train and Seth's adrenalin was pumping with excitement to deliver his lecture. It was a short-distance walk to Lund University campus, which was beautifully landscaped with very old giant fir trees. It was shortly after the noon hour and already a large crowd of people was starting to gather in front of the auditorium. Seth was pleased so many were planning to attend his lecture; but adversely, the huge crowd would make it difficult for Karl to find him… and he had to give the duffel bag to Karl before the lecture. Seth decided to stand beside one of the giant trees at the end of the very long sidewalk to the entrance and cradled the duffel bag in his arms in a conspicuous position. Nils stood away at a distance with bent knee and his foot propped up leaning against a tree farther down the sidewalk. They did not want to appear they were together.

It was only a short time later when they noticed a rather tall, muscular-built young man pacing from one area of the campus to another, mingling with the crowd, but stopping to talk to no one. On the second trip around campus, the young man stopped in front of Seth to talk.

"Are you going to stay for the lecture?" He asked.

With a smile and a quick answer, Seth replied, "I guess I have to… I'm the guest speaker."

"Well, then," the young man informed, "I'm Karl Larsson."

"Are you a student here?" Seth asked.

"No," he answered.

Seth forced the password to be answered and asked, "What university did you attend?"

Karl was quick to respond, "Wash U."

The two shook hands and Seth immediately gave him the duffel bag.

Nils came forward to shake his hand, also, and asked, "Will we see you again?"

Karl looked around the campus and volunteered, "Yes, Fritz and I will wait for both of you after the lecture. Let's meet here at this same tree." Karl vanished quickly into the crowd.

Nils started to chuckle, "If I have ever seen a Viking, he is one. Hell, his shoulders are twice my size and his biceps… wow! I'm glad he's on our side."

———

Seth's lecture on urban design, land-use planning and urban sprawl was a timely study for Sweden as the country was experiencing an influx of emigrants from Turkey and the Middle East. The auditorium was filled to capacity and his lecture was well accepted. From the many questions asked after the lecture, it was evident the topic of utilizing every square foot of land available to its potential for population growth was extremely important to Sweden.

———

The Swedes were reminded of the early ninth century when the Scandinavian Vikings had to turn to the sea in search of food to feed families of eight or nine children, which were common. Rich farmland was at a premium as very large estates were owned by the royal families and the extremely wealthy. This combined with a short growing season made it impossible to produce enough food to feed the fast growing population. The restless, young landless Norsemen were forced to seek their fortunes elsewhere and became seafaring wanderers of merchants... many were skilled craftsmen looking for foreign markets. They wove a pattern of trade and exploration, which stretched across the oceans from Russia to Turkey to Canada and to far distant countries as China and Afghanistan. They had the best iron in the world for making weapons with sharp edges on the blades and an ample supply of timber for building ships that could sail across the seas. They had a variety of ships especially built to handle a specific need: a fishing boat, cargo ship, warship and a raider boat. The longboat with its special keel and rudder built to accommodate shallow water could anchor on a beach, thereby allowing the men to advance swiftly for a coastal invasion of a village or monastery. With the unique design of the hull, the marauding longboat could alter directions quickly by changing the position of the oars. They were seafarers extraordinaire.

They were adept at raiding as they were at trading, and some Norsemen found it was easier to plunder the small villages and monasteries as they were poorly fortified from invasion. They killed; they kidnapped; they plundered, and they took slaves. The most feared of all the Vikings were the berserkers, who induced drugs such as the hallucinogenic mushroom or consumed massive amounts of alcohol to dull their senses rendering them impervious to pain.

They became maniacal with uncontrollable frenzy; and unless the berserker was mortally wounded immediately, he would continue to fight, charging with every thrust of his battle ax.

The Vikings were adventurers who sailed the seas without boundaries, but they were not a conquering people. Some assimilated into the societies they occupied, sharing cultural advancements and learning from each other. Some traveled with their wife and family seeking a warmer climate and an abundance of food. The old metaphorical adage declares: If you track the descent of your family lineage back far enough, you will find a Viking.

———

When there were no more questions, the auditorium emptied quickly. Seth hurriedly gathered his notes from the podium and prepared to leave the stage. He gave a sigh of relief, as public speaking is not one of his favorite things to do; but to his chagrin, he realizes if he is to become an internationally well-known architect, he will be called upon to give many lectures.

The auditorium was empty with the exception of a few stragglers far to the back of the room. Seth could not believe his eyes when he recognized the odd couple in the last row and the tour guide four aisles in front of them. He scurried out the side door hoping no one would follow. *The scene reminded him of Hong Kong, when he ran down the long peer in Victoria Harbor to elude members of the Chinese Triad.* He saw the giant fir tree where he was to meet Fritz, Carl and Nils, but no one was there. He decided to relax at the tree and wait to see what would happen. Within two minutes the tour guide approached him: "It was a very interesting lecture and I'm glad I came." He looked all around as if scouting the area and said, "It's fun to be back on campus."

Seth inquired, "Are you interested in architecture?"

"Oh, I dabble in the field of structural engineering during the off-season for tourists. Right now, I can make more money as a tour guide."

Nothing was said for a few minutes, when the tour guide asked, "Was that your duffel bag I saw in the auditorium or was it a coincidence that another man has one just like yours?"

With a surprised, high pitched voice, Seth answered, "Really? My bag is in my room at the hotel." He paused and chuckled, "It's protecting a very expensive Kosta vase in bubble wrap.

"Can I give you a lift back to your hotel?" The tour guide volunteered.

"Thanks, but I bought a return ticket on the train and I plan to meet my friend Nils here in a few minutes."

The two looked at one another; both nodded; and said good-bye.

Seth sat on a bench beside the tree and waited… and waited. Finally, after an hour, Nils almost ran down the long sidewalk.

"Where have you been… and where are Fritz and Karl?" Seth was agitated. "I almost gave up on you!"

In a breathless, excited voice, Nills began, "It's been a very busy afternoon and you won't believe what we have learned about the odd couple and the tour guide. Fritz, Karl and I spotted the three of them immediately and decided to do a little investigating of our own." Nils talked in a very clever, know-it-all voice, "Are you ready for this?"

"Shoot!"

"The tour guide was easy to track down. We called the tourist office and found out he was hired and trained a couple of days ago and he has already given notice that he is quitting."

Seth mentioned, "Well, he said he was getting bored with the job. Maybe, it's just coincidental."

"Okay, we'll give him the benefit of a doubt." Nils continued, "The odd couple was a little more difficult to trace. We were lucky Fritz has clout in Malmo; and with the help of the hotel concierge, we found out they are traveling on an Italian passport… from Naples to be exact. They have open reservations at the hotel with no definite departure date." Nils scratched the back of his head thinking aloud, "The couple could be waiting for us to check out of the hotel and then continue to follow us."

"That's a possibility. We'll just have to be careful," Seth volunteered.

The two were quiet for a few minutes trying to digest this information when Seth realized Fritz and Karl were not with Nils. "I thought we were going to meet with Fritz so he can explain why he involved us in this mystery for the urgent need for secrecy in giving Karl the architectural drawings, and whatever else is in the packet he put in my duffel bag."

Nils answered, "Fritz wants us to meet him right away at his uncle's apartment at 31 Freisgaten Street, which is close to Folketspark."

"Okay," and requested, "first let's stop at the hotel so I can drop off my lecture notes and grab a snack to eat before we go."

Nils was fast to answer, "Sounds like a plan to me."

———

The return train ride to Malmo was uneventful with both young men at rest with their eyes closed and engrossed in their own thoughts.

Seth had received an invitation to lecture at Lund University four months prior to the date and was excited to be acknowledged in his field of architecture. He planned a nice vacation for him and Rachel as a second honeymoon and he purchased a beautiful Rolex watch to give her the night before the trip to celebrate the occasion. He languished in his thoughts… wanting to hold Rachel in his arms and smother her with kisses. The pain rippled through his body as he realizes she is in China and he is riding a train in Sweden. He feels inside his coat jacket for the watch, which is still nestled deeply in the pocket and remembers he forgot to leave it at home. He silently verbalizes… slowly: *She is a million miles away.*

Nils opened his eyes to ask, "Who's a million miles away?"

Not realizing he spoke the words, Seth answered, "Rachel." That's all he said and volunteered nothing more and Nils closed his eyes.

———

It was late afternoon when Seth and Nils returned to the hotel. They were surprised to find the door to their room closed, but not locked. The room had been ransacked. Both their suitcases were placed on the bed with the contents in a rumpled heap on the floor. Seth turned to look for the expensive Kosta vase and saw it on the desk beside the bed minus the bubble wrap. He thought: *At least the intruder did not break the vase.*

They straightened the room and thoroughly checked to see if anything had been stolen, but nothing was missing. They surmised the intruder was looking for the duffel bag and/or its contents.

With a fast stride, Seth and Nils walked through the crowded hotel lobby and out the door to hail a cab for their meeting with Fritz. Everything was getting too close and personal for their liking and they wanted some answers right away.

They did not see the odd couple sitting in a dark corner of the lobby.

Chapter Six

S unrays cast forth late afternoon shadows from trees and with the
lack of sufficient street lights in the old section of town, the cab
driver found it difficult to locate 31 Freisgaten Street. Finally, the cab
stopped in front of a very old apartment building; Seth paid the cab
fare and Fritz opened the door to greet them. After he introduced Seth
and Nils to his uncle, who is a supervisor of structural engineering
for a large company in Malmo, they joined Karl in the dining room
where he was studying a large spate of blueprints, which was strewn
across the table.

Fritz apologized to Seth for not hearing his lecture and explained,
"I guess Nils told you we decided to do a little investigating ourselves
and I'm glad we did." Fritz turned to Nils clarifying, "After you left
us to meet Seth, Karl and I found out the tour guide is employed by an
engineering firm in Denmark to spy on competing, rival companies
that have new and innovative designs with a greater potential for
success in the market, but who have not yet acquired patents or
copyrights. I guess we could call him a pirate of industry."

With a feeling of pride and approval, the uncle looked around the
table at the four young men, who exemplify quality craftsmen in their
fields of design... civil, structural, mechanical, and architectural...
and acknowledged, "I guess our secret for designing a workable
solution to build a means for connecting Malmo, Sweden and
Copenhagen, Denmark is well-known in the industry by now." He

emphatically stated, "We have to get these blueprints to our lawyers in Denmark. They have to be submitted to the government patent and trademark offices as quickly as possible."

Karl spoke, "I know there are several companies in Denmark that are working on similar plans for this project; and these companies are offering huge bonuses and incentives to the designers who can come up with a viable plan. The awards and prestige that this project will bring to the company or companies are unfathomable... and speed is of the essence."

"You're right!" Nils injected. "The gossip around the water cooler where I work is there are French engineers and an American group of engineers who have joined efforts to form a Channel Tunnel Study to connect France and England via the English Channel. From what we have been told, their designs will deal with strong tides and a chalk-like base, which dips steeply near the coast."

The uncle stated: "Well, we certainly have our problems. Malmo's bedrock consists of lime and flint with many water-filled fissures; and the rock will have to be removed using rotary cutters and picks. Precise control measurements must be taken to ensure the temporary support construction does not move, and the measuring requires extreme accuracy; and the list goes on and on." He stopped to marvel at what this project will provide to the area and continued, "When completed, it will combine a two-track rail crossing and a four-lane road bridge over the Oresund Strait via Europe's longest suspension bridge, an artificial island and the world's largest immersed tunnel." Once again he stopped, rubbed his hands together vigorously and proclaimed, "Now, gentlemen, many of our brightest designers have combined their talents to create this huge project; this marvelous feat of engineering... and to think we have the blueprints in front of us on this table."

The men stood mesmerized staring at the assortment of blueprints. Realization of the enormous amount of man-hours it took to create this project was almost unbelievable. The uncle reminded the group: "It was with the dual cooperation of both countries... financially and politically... that made it all happen. Once the construction starts, the project will mean hundreds of jobs, which will boost our economy and it will take quite a few years to complete."

Fritz and Karl looked at one another with a feeling of pride, as they know they are a small cog in the big wheel. They have contributed their share toward creating this monument, which will stand the test of time in history.

Seth bounced out of his trance and blurted, "Oh, I almost forgot! Our hotel room was ransacked while we were in Lund. Nothing was taken, but I am sure the intruder was looking for my blue duffel bag." He reported, "The tour guide talked to me before the lecture and made mention of my bag and said he noticed a similar one on campus and asked if it were mine. I told him 'no' that I left mine back at the hotel. I believe he has an accomplice who searched our room."

Fritz responded, "Well, we know the odd couple did not do it, because they sat in the auditorium the whole time listening to the lecture." With a discouraged thought, "I guess there are more spies involved than we want to believe. We have to figure out a way to get these plans to Denmark, safely."

The uncle suggested, "For now, they are safe here in my apartment. If you noticed, my windows have bars on them, which make us feel safer living in this part of town. With two children in college, I feel this is all I can afford; and my wife says she will live wherever I want to live." His lips curled to a smile and he quietly adds, "We are still in love after twenty-nine years."

Seth felt a pang of jealousy as his thoughts immediately went to Rachel. *Why did she have to leave? Doesn't she love me! His wife is here by his side in this old apartment and Rachel gave up a mansion to live in China. I wish I could take back that horrible night we argued. I love her so much it hurts.*

Fritz was the first one to suggest, and all four men agreed, the duffel bag was no longer of value to transport the plans. Its function had been compromised and they pondered the thought: *the tour guide, his accomplice, the odd couple and whoever else may be spying on them are aware another means of concealment will have to be found for the plans to be transported to Denmark.*

Seth was the first one to remind the group he is leaving Malmo Monday, day after tomorrow, and is planning to fly from Copenhagen to the States. His mode of transportation from Malmo to Copenhagen will be by ferryboat across the Oresund Strait.

Karl quickly suggested, "I have to return home to Copenhagen also on Monday and I could travel with Seth. But we have to find some means of hiding the plans in something we could carry and not look suspicious."

The uncle spoke: "I think I may have an idea to solve our problem." He called to his wife who was cooking dinner in the kitchen to come to the dining room. He asked: "Dear, do you think the posters you have made to advertise our sons' musical performance at the Malmo Festival for Sunday night are large enough to hide all these plans behind them in the frames?"

"Oh, yes, easily with no problem. Let me get them."

Everyone was amazed to see four colorful, large posters advertising times and dates of performances in Malmo and Copenhagen of the musical group *Slick Sound of Tomorrow… from Sweden.* The uncle proudly explained, "My wife painted these beautiful posters, which will be placed on the stage when the band performs. My sons have made arrangements for a truck to pick them up, along with these posters and their instruments, tomorrow morning to take them into the Malmo central district where they, along with six friends, will entertain Sunday night. The band also has been invited to play Monday night in Copenhagen at Tivoli Garden." With a concerned thought, the uncle mentioned, "The only problem, as I see it, is transferring the large posters by ferryboat to Copenhagen."

The wife injected, "Oh, no. Our sons were not going to use the posters at Tivoli Garden, because it would be too expensive to ship them from Malmo to Copenhagen and the ferryboat does not carry cargo of any kind… just passengers."

"Well, at least we can get the blueprints out of this apartment and into Malmo," Fritz half-heartedly spoke. "I'm sure we can come up with an idea to get them to Copenhagen."

They all stood quietly for awhile, each one mulling over various ideas in their own mind, but not expressing anything. Fritz suggested, "Why don't we meet tomorrow at the Flea Market about noon. With the additional tourists in town for the Malmo Festival, the area will be swarming with shoppers and we can blend in with the crowd."

Nils was quick to say, "Sounds like a plan to me." And everyone agreed.

"How about I give you and Seth a ride back to your hotel," Fritz volunteered.

At the last minute, Seth remembered to take his duffel bag, and concealed it as best he could by rolling it tightly and putting it in a large paper bag with a wool-knit scarf flowing out the top. This was Fritz's idea, as he explained someone may be spying on the apartment.

Nils and Seth looked at one another with eyebrows raised thinking: *Fritz definitely has a flair for the dramatic.*

The four men scampered down the apartment stairs to Fritz's car, which was parked a good distance away, but no one paid any attention to the old truck parked across the street. The odd couple peered out the truck window from a scrunched sitting position and watched the men leave.

Chapter Seven

The distance from the uncle's apartment to the hotel was not very far, but Fritz found it difficult to find streets that had not been closed for the Malmo Festival. Saturday night revelers were out in full swing enjoying entertainment on every street corner. They danced and they sang. Shoppers meandered slowly through the streets to purchase special items made from other countries, which boasted their cultural designs.

Fritz took a circuitous route around the festival and stopped the car in front of a modest home with a small bronze bust of a man resting on a pedestal. In a nostalgic mood, Fritz lamented, "This is Per Albin Hansson's home. It certainly isn't impressive considering he served as Prime Minister of Sweden for many years." Fritz shook his head in amazement, "I find it very interesting my grandfather and Per Albin died the same year... 1946. They were good friends with the same political ideology for a better Sweden. I wonder if it was God's plan both friends should die in the same year."

The four men sat quietly in the car looking at the unpretentious home when Nils asked, "Are they buried in the same cemetery?"

"No." Fritz answered and explained, "When they were young and worked together for a better Sweden, as I mentioned before, my grandfather worked as a custom's officer, which was a position staffed by the king. When the king realized my grandfather was involved with the social democratic movement, he fired and blackballed him from obtaining any other employment. Per Albin was safe from the king's wrath, because he worked for the party paper. Grandfather had no choice but to leave Sweden so he could support his family. With the aid of his sister who lived in the United States, my grandfather, grandmother, my dad and his sister left Malmo and emigrated to United States in 1913... Missouri to be exact."

Karl, Nils and Seth realized Fritz was in his element of enjoyment, which is talking about the history of his family. They decided it was better to sit and listen, while Fritz was happy to continue the story. "My dad was nine years old at the time when the family left Sweden and has always enjoyed telling the story of their crossing the Atlantic Ocean. They boarded the *Mauretania,* which was a sister ship to the *Titanic,* in Liverpool, England and sailed for the United States. When the ship sailed over the exact latitude and longitude of ocean where the *Titanic* sank, the captain called for all engines to stop in reverence to those who died. It was exactly one year earlier to the date on April 14, 1912 that the passenger liner, *Titanic,* sank taking over fifteen hundred passengers to a watery grave. At this time of year in the North Atlantic shipping lanes, the captain has to be careful of icebergs that can float just under the surface of the water. The *Titanic* was built to be unsinkable; but at a speed of 22 knots, the ship collided with a submerged iceberg, ripping a large gash in the side of the ship."

Fritz started the car and continued to tell the story as they slowly moved toward the hotel. "All passengers were invited to be on their respective deck for the ceremony. The *Mauretania* remained at a full stop while the captain of the ship tossed a huge wreath of colorful flowers over the side of the ship and offered prayers. It was customary for each passenger deck to have its own band of musicians and the captain asked all bands to play 'Nearer My God to Thee'."

Before Fritz could realize where he was driving, the car automatically turned into the hotel parking lot. He was happily surprised he could drive and tell an emotional story at the same time. He turned to his companions and apologized, "I'm sorry for the long speech. I can get carried away when I talk about my family."

Nils approvingly said, "Rightfully so. That's quite a story." With a silly smirk added, "My family keeps all our relatives locked in the closet. We're trying to forget our past. We must have a few berserkers hanging on our family tree. Hell, we don't even celebrate birthdays."

Karl teased, "Nils, you may be older than you think."

The four companions laughed and gave no thought to the serious problem before them. Seth and Nils jumped out of the car quickly calling a hasty "see ya tomorrow at noon."

Seth tucked the big paper bag containing the duffel bag under his arm as the two proceeded to walk through the lobby, looking for the odd couple and anyone else who looked suspicious. They were happy to see their hotel room door securely locked. Seth placed the big paper bag on his bed and proceeded to take out the wool-knit scarf and the tightly rolled blue duffel bag. He breathed a sigh of relief, "I guess no spies followed us," and in a dry facetious wit suggested to Nils, "I think we are becoming melodramatic like Fritz. What do you say we join the revelers for some fun tonight after we have a bite to eat?"

"Sounds like a plan!"

———

The Saturday night crowd was loud and rambunctious with everyone enjoying the festivities. It reminded Seth of the celebrations in Hong Kong, which sparked his memory of Rachel when she was kidnapped during a parade. That is a part of his life he would like to forget: Rachel was taken to Yokohama, Japan where she was held for ransom and Seth was a soldier on the frontline in Korea. He remembered he was asked to assist with her capture, which was successful, during his rest and recuperation leave in Yokohama. He becomes sentimental with maudlin thoughts that their life together has been a series of terrifying events… over which they had no control. He thinks: *I can control our situation, now. There is no need for us to be separated. My love for Rachel extends all boundaries; and if I have to live in China, that is what I will do. I'll call my dad tomorrow to find out if he has heard from her.*

Nils noticed Seth became very quiet and asked, "Are you thinking of your wife, again? I can always tell because you get very quiet."

"Yes, I was." Seth answered. He looked at his watch and noticed it is twelve midnight. *Rachel, I'm sorry. I missed ten o'clock by two hours. Forgive me. I love you.* He suggested to Nils, "Let's head back to our hotel. It's getting late."

"Hey, man, we can sleep late tomorrow morning. We don't have to meet the guys until noon and we definitely want to walk to the harbor area to see the Tall Ships," Nils pleaded and continued, "Ships of all sizes and designs started sailing into port late today for the Tall Ships Race," and asked, "are you familiar with the event?"

"I've read about the races in magazines and have seen pictures of them, but I, personally, never have seen the ships." Seth replied.

In a pundit style, Nils began: "The International Fleets of Tall Ships are ambassadors for their respective countries and visit selected ports throughout the world during the race. The great flotilla is an ocean-racing tradition that began in the age of the tea clippers. The ships are different in size and style with some masts towering to 250 feet above the waterline. It's really a memorable experience to see them, and Malmo is lucky to have been selected as one of the ports of call. When the ships reach the final port, there is a Grand Parade of Sail where the Tall Ships pass crowds of spectators as they leave to sail for their home ports."

The two men continued their slow pace, pushing through the crowd enjoying the music from the many bands along the way to the harbor area. They could see the tall masts in the distance; and when they walked closer to the ships, the atmosphere became more vibrant and alive with people enjoying this memorable experience. The ships are in port for the Malmo Festival and the race is to begin Monday.

Seth could not believe his eyes when he gazed down the long pier and saw a ship he thought he would never see again.

"I don't believe it! It's the *Ladybug!*" Seth yelled. "Nils, come on." Seth started to run.

Nils cracked up with laughter and breathlessly called to Seth while trying to keep up with his fast pace, "What is so exciting about seeing a ladybug. Those little bugs are all over Sweden. They're our symbol for good luck. My grandmother told me you should never hurt one."

Seth pointed to the cargo ship, which is a tramp steamer, at the end of the pier. "There it is! I'm talking about that ship." He stopped at the gang plank and turned to Nils with a big smile, "You're right! The *Ladybug* was my good luck when I was in China."

Nils posed the question, "You are going to have to tell me about your experiences in China sometime?"

"Okay. It's a long story. Perhaps... later."

Seth called to the seaman on deck, asking if he could see the captain of the ship. "Please tell him it's Seth Coleman who traveled as a passenger on the *Ladybug* from Le Havre, France to Hong Kong, China.

The seaman was gone for only a few minutes when two men returned to the deck. Captain Oscarson burst forth with a deep loud happy voice, "Seth, my boy, I never thought I would ever see you again... and here you are in my home town. What brings you to Malmo?"

Captain Oscarson embraced Seth in a fatherly hug with tears filling his rheumy eyes with joy. He pulled away from Seth to take a long look at a young man who once was his protégé while sailing on his ship. "You look a little older, but I guess war will do that to you...and," he paused and laughed, "marriage can make you look older sometimes. It's been a few years."

Seth believed Captain Oscarson was his surrogate father during his wild adventure to China aboard the *Ladybug*. With a warm feeling of respect, Seth informed, "Well, first there was the Korean War, which I managed to survive; and then I got married, which I'm hoping to survive. My wife Rachel and I had a terrible argument a few days ago and she returned to the Island of Lantau to be with her father and the children in the orphanage."

The captain counseled, "Sometimes things happen to disrupt a marriage; but you'll see, she will come to her senses. I remember General von Horstmann's daughter Rachel very well... she is a beautiful woman."

Seth introduced his friend Nils to the captain and the three retired to the break room where they could sit and talk over a vodka martini. The captain asked again, "Seth, tell me. What brings you to Malmo?"

"If you remember when I was aboard your ship, I mentioned that I had just graduated from college with a master's degree in architecture. Well, when I returned home from China, I was drafted into the Korean War; and after I was mustered out of service, I married Rachel. My career as an architect with Joseph A Gabriel and Son really jump started when I designed a project for south-side Chicago and wrote an article on the project for an international architectural magazine. A professor at Lund University was interested in the project and invited me to talk on the subject. I was excited to receive the offer to lecture at such a prestigious university and I made plans for Rachel and me to travel together, making the trip to Sweden like a second honeymoon. The lecture went very well this morning… but the second honeymoon fizzled." Seth hung his head with his eyes to the floor and remained quiet in his own thoughts.

The captain tried to turn his thoughts to a happier subject and mentioned, "You always said you wanted to become a famous architect and design beautiful buildings which will stand the test of time like Notre Dame in Paris."

With a feeling of depression, Seth uttered, "My time in Paris seems like a million years ago."

The captain turned to Nils and asked, "I assume you are a friend of Seth's?"

Nils was quick to reply, "Yes, I am also an architect. We graduated from the same college in the States, but my home is in Stockholm."

The conversation turned quickly to reminiscing about the events aboard the *Ladybug* while the ship traversed the oceans from Le Havre to Hong Kong. Nils sat quietly enjoying the story about Seth's harrowing experiences in the Orient; but it was two o'clock in the morning and the late hour was catching up with their lack of sleep. The two young men took turns yawning and regretfully decided they had to leave. The captain escorted the two young men to the top deck to say their good-byes with the desire to keep in touch; and once again Seth gave the captain a fatherly hug. Nils could easily see the two were closer than friends and he hoped some day Seth would tell him the complete story about his trip to China.

It had been a long, exhausting day; and after visiting with Captain Oscarson, they completely forgot the noon meeting at the Flea Market, when the serious problem of transferring the blueprints to Denmark had to be reconciled.

———

The large crowd had dispersed leaving only a few stragglers to wander down the pier. There was a full moon, which brightly painted a beautiful silhouette of the Tall Ships resting in the harbor with only small waves lapping at the wharf. As Seth and Nils started to walk down the gangplank to disembark the *Ladybug,* Seth turned to Nils with a frightful look on his face. Captain Oscarson called in a raspy tone of voice to Seth, "I remember you had that same look on your face when the Chinese Triad hoodlums tried to board the *Ladybug* while it was at anchor in the harbor in Macau. What do you see?"

Seth spoke to Nils, "Look down the pier. It's the odd couple! The man's wearing that sweatshirt and the woman has that blue and yellow cap on her head."

Nils and Seth quickly ran back up the gangplank and sat down on the deck by the railing. Captain Oscarson looked at them both cowering low as if hiding from a menacing foe.

"What's this all about, Seth? What are you doing?" The captain demanded.

In an urgent tone, as if pleading for help, Seth looked at the captain saying, "I think it is imperative that we talk."

The three men returned to the break room where Seth told the captain the whole story with alacrity as he perceived the situation: the need for secrecy in transferring the blueprints of an Oresund Bridge from Malmo to Copenhagen; their concern for the spies who have been following them from Christinehof Slot to Malmo; their plan to hide the blueprints behind large posters, which will be transported to Copenhagen.

With a worried expression, Seth emphasized, "Our plan stopped when we could not figure how to get the posters from the stage after the band's performance Sunday night in Malmo to Copenhagen since the ferryboat will not transport cargo."

The captain listened intently, but said nothing.

Seth's countenance brightened with a positive thought, "The plan is ideal! The musicians are playing in Tivoli Garden Monday and the spies will believe the posters are essential to publicize the concert. Hopefully, they will not realize the posters are concealing the blueprints."

Seth hastened to add, "We have to come up with a solution fast… by tomorrow night… or I should say tonight. We are all meeting at noon today to discuss a viable solution, if there is one."

With a broad grin, the captain joyfully suggested, "I just may have the solution to your problem," and gently slapped Seth on the back.

Seth's euphoric expression said it all. "What do you mean?"

"I have to leave port very early Monday morning to accommodate the Tall Ships Race. If you can get the posters to the *Ladybug* by four o'clock Monday morning, I'll be happy to transport them to Copenhagen."

Seth gave the captain another big hug expressing his thanks, "We'll have the posters here by four o'clock," thinking: *He will always be my surrogate father. I am truly blessed.*

Nils felt the heartrending emotions between the two. He stomped his foot while swinging his arms in disbelief, "This ship is truly good luck!"

In a philosophical mood, the captain murmured, "Yes, good fortune comes to him who believes."

Captain Oscarson returned to the top deck and slowly scanned the immediate wharf area for the odd couple. There was no one on the dock. With a wave of his hand, he motioned the two men to leave the ship.

Chapter Eight
Earlier Saturday Night

After Fritz and Karl dropped off Seth and Nils at the hotel, they decided not to spend Saturday night at the Malmo Festival. They stopped at a restaurant for a hearty supper and returned immediately to the uncle's apartment. They were anxious to put the blueprints behind the posters and have them ready for pickup Sunday morning. When they arrived, there were two police cars parked at the curb and neighbors were standing on the lawn seeking information about the robbery at Apartment #31. They ran up the stairs, but were stopped at the door by a policeman who asked for their identity. Fritz explained he and his friend were staying the night at his uncle's house and after they showed identification, they were allowed to enter the apartment. They were apprehensive not knowing what to expect as they carefully stepped over the clutter of things on the living room floor. They breathed a sigh of relief when they noticed the four posters were still leaning against the dining room wall where they had left them, and they were happy to see the uncle and aunt in the kitchen talking to a policeman. The uncle was extremely nervous, but he tried to maintain a sense of rationality while explaining what happened.

"It's an evening routine... I take my dog Thor, a Siberian husky, for a run around the neighborhood. The two of us left the apartment... and I don't lock the door because we are never gone very long. Tonight, I changed our routine and Thor and I ran through

Folketspark. I always hesitate to take Thor there because of the tall pine trees, which deposit large patches of pine needles on the ground. Well, Thor ran through a thick patch and one very large needle became wedged in his paw. Thor hobbled home as best he could... howling with pain... trying to walk. We were only gone about ten or maybe fifteen minutes. We were about a half block away from the apartment, when I saw two men run down the stairs and hop into a car, which was parked at the curb. I did not recognize either man, and I did not think to get the license number. I was frightened for my wife who was in the apartment alone and I could think of nothing else, but to rush inside to see if she was okay.

"I found my wife in the kitchen tied to a chair. I untied her and was satisfied she was not physically hurt, but you can see she is emotionally stressed. She explained the two men violently pushed the door open... probably thinking the door was locked. They hurriedly went through all the rooms looking for something... pulling drawers open; looking in cupboards and closets; yanking pillow cushions from the sofa; taking the mattresses off the beds... well, you can see the mess they made. When the burglars heard the dog yelping, and saw we were coming home, they ran out the door... and then you arrived."

The officer asked, "Do you have any idea why they riffled your apartment and can you tell if they took anything?"

The uncle emphatically answered, "I have no idea what they were looking for or why they would break into our apartment. We have nothing of any real value. My wife and I will have to straighten up this mess before we know if something is missing."

The officer turned to the wife with an apology for her distress, but had to interrogate her at this time. "Would you please tell me what happened."

The wife's voice was almost inaudible; her whole body continued to shake with fear, and she began: "They pushed their way into the room, grabbed me immediately and spun me around so I couldn't see their face. They tied me to this chair and told me to be quiet and I would not be hurt. I obeyed! I was really scared!"

The officer asked, "So... you can't describe them... How tall? Hair color? Clothes? Anything?"

"No. Nothing." She paused briefly to absorb what had just happened and slowly mentioned, "There was one thing. One of the men had a dry cough. You know, like a nervous cough."

The officer acknowledged, "Well, that's something, I guess."

Fritz and Karl sat quietly listening to the officer interrogate his uncle and aunt and volunteered nothing and hoped they would not mention the blueprints.

The officer tried to console the couple and assured them they would keep a close watch over the neighborhood.

After the police left, the neighbors were quickly apprised of the burglary and informed nothing was stolen and no one was hurt. They all offered their assistance, if it were ever needed and returned to their apartment. The uncle hugged his wife with the consoling thought: *no one was hurt,* and collapsed in a chair from exhaustion and excitement.

Fritz immediately apologized to his aunt and uncle, "I'm sorry I have involved you in the Oresund bridge project. I have heard stories of industrial pirates terrorizing people while invading offices and homes to get what they want; but thankfully, I know of no one who has ever been killed. They are vicious, but they are not killers."

The uncle acknowledged the apology with a shake of his head and closed his eyes in disbelief at the whirlwind of havoc wreaked by the burglars. Fritz and Karl remained quiet in respect for the uncle's dazed state of mind, hoping the violence would not escalate. They were happy no one was physically hurt and pleased to see the aunt was beginning to gain her composure… but no one spoke. The silence was broken when they heard Thor whimpering softly in his bed by the backdoor.

The uncle jumped out of the chair when he heard his dog and in a pathetic voice whispered, "I'm sorry I forgot about you." He searched for the tweezers, but could not find them in the rumpled mess in all the rooms. He became extremely frustrated, but then remembered the tool box under the kitchen sink. He grabbed a pair of pliers and with a gentle, compassionate touch he pulled the needle from Thor's paw and whispered, "good, boy". Thor showed his appreciation by nuzzling closer to his master.

Karl asked hoping for the right answer, "Please tell me the blueprints are safe somewhere?"

The uncle gently soothed his dog while he spoke, "It's a stroke of luck! Yes, they're safe!" He explained: "After you, Fritz, Seth and Nils left this afternoon, something told me we should tend to the blueprints right away. My sons had to leave to rehearse with the band for their upcoming concerts in Malmo and Copenhagen, but I asked them to stay a little longer to help us affix the blueprints on a thin sheet of plywood. We set the poster board on top and used a large heavy frame to hold everything in place. Since we had purchased all the materials earlier, the job was done rather quickly and we were satisfied the blueprints were protected. I'm glad I listened to my gut feeling."

Everyone turned to look at the four posters leaning against the wall. Karl surmised, "I think sometimes it is better to hide something in clear view. It is only natural not to check the obvious place."

Karl studied the posters and complimented the aunt, "These posters are really a work of art. Each one depicts a popular scene of Sweden with the advertisement message of the band's schedules within the design. I estimate the posters are about five feet by seven feet. Is that right?"

The aunt proudly replied, "Yes. I want them to be easily seen from a distance and they will provide color on the stage. Most performing musicians use green plants or some dingy backdrops; and being an art teacher, I was inspired to paint these posters for my sons' band. Both of their concerts are outdoors and I'm hoping these posters will draw a big audience."

Their conversation was interrupted when the two sons returned home after rehearsing with the band. The sons were horrified to see what the burglars had done to the apartment, but they were pleased no one was harmed and the large posters had not been disturbed. Each one took turns telling them the story of the attempted burglary. When Fritz' aunt mentioned one of the burglars had a nervous cough, it sparked his memory and he looked at Karl posing the question, "When Seth, Nils and I had lunch the other day at Christinehof with the tour guide, he coughed many times through lunch, but I thought he had a cold or something. Maybe, he is one of the spies. Maybe, he is the burglar with the nervous cough."

Karl critically suggested, "Hell, Fritz, I think you're jumping to a conclusion!"

"Damn it, Karl, you weren't there!" Fritz became adamant, "He had been a tour guide for only a few days and quit after Seth and Nils took the tour. That's more than coincidental!"

The uncle could see everyone was getting tired and testy and suggested, "Let's straighten up the apartment a little bit and make the beds so we can all get some sleep. I think tomorrow will be a busy day. The truck will be here at ten o'clock in the morning to pick up the posters, the instruments and the sound system."

The son informed, "Yes, that's right. We are going to follow the truck in our car and the band members will meet us at the stage in Malmo at eleven to help us set up everything. The sound system always takes quite a bit of time."

Karl was quick to add, "If it's okay with you, I would like to ride in the truck with the posters," and suggested, "Fritz, you can drive your car and meet us at the stage."

Fritz agreed, "Okay, then we will meet Seth and Nils at noon at the Flea Market." All of a sudden with a perplexing thought Fritz yelled, "Hell, we haven't taken time to think how we are going to get the posters to Copenhagen."

Everyone was startled with the reality of the problem which had to be solved, immediately, but no one said anything. The room was quiet for a long time with no one volunteering any suggestions when the hall clock chimed two. The uncle rubbed his bleary eyes and declared once again, "It's two o'clock in the morning and we are all tired and we all need some sleep! Try to find a comfortable place wherever you can in all this mess and we will talk in the morning."

Chapter Nine

T he mid-morning sun shone brightly through the window in Seth's room casting rays of light onto his bed, forcing him to awake. He turned slowly removing the glare of the sun while regretting his salacious dream of Rachel was interrupted. He closed his eyes again hoping to recapture the dream. It was so real he could feel her presence. He stretched his arm across the bed to touch the soft curves of her body with his gentle callused hand… regretting it was only a dream. He languished awhile longer reliving many romantic interludes and with a whimsical smile he glances at his finger where there is a slight scar. He gently rubbed the scar and recalled the afternoon he and Rachel pledged their love by cutting their fingers and pressing the small cuts together, theoretically making them blood lovers. His lips curled to a broad smile as he remembered he never told Rachel he purposely irritated the cut so it would not heal properly in order to make a scar. He will always remember that afternoon. He glanced out the window to see the sun is now higher in the sky and reluctantly puts these loving memories out of his mind. With the discouraging thought, he knows he must confront reality… Rachel is in China.

He fortified his energy to get out of bed when he remembered he wanted to phone his dad to learn if he had heard from Rachel. But then realized, he would have to wait until late afternoon to make the call, because of the time difference between Sweden and the States. Totally discouraged, he flopped down in bed hitting the back of his head hard against the headboard complaining, "Damn, that hurts!"

The commotion aroused Nils, who really wanted to ignore Seth and go back to sleep, but his curiosity stimulated some sense of life in his body and he rubbed his eyes, mumbling, "That was sure a short night's sleep!"

Seth started to laugh when he stared at Nils who looked painfully pathetic. "You've never been in the military, have you? You learn to catch sleep wherever and whenever you can."

In a comical rebuttal, Nils replied, "Well, that doesn't make me want to enlist! I feel like death warmed over," and pleaded, "It can't be time to get up?"

Seth good-naturedly advised, "If we hustle, we can get some breakfast before we meet Fritz and Karl at the Flea Market at noon."

———

The hotel lobby was bustling with activity with tour groups assembling for their morning excursions. Tourists were anxious to see the Tall Ships, which had anchored in the harbor over night, and conversations reverberated with excitement to start the day's festivities. The hotel dining room was rather sparse of diners as most had eaten an early breakfast, but there were a few late stragglers like Seth and Nils who were enjoying an early brunch.

It took two cups of coffee and a hearty meal to awaken their senses to stimulate conversation. They discussed the events of the previous two days, which had made their life a little chaotic. Seth's venture in Sweden to lecture at Lund University turned into an "adventure" when they agreed to meet Fritz at Christinehof. They did not realize the magnitude of his simple request to deliver blueprints to Karl in Lund would involve them in a full-blown espionage caper.

Their late-night rendezvous with Captain Oscarson of the *Ladybug* was discussed at great length, acknowledging it is a stroke of good luck the ship will be able to transport the posters to Copenhagen. Both men are anxious to report the good news to Fritz when they meet at noon.

Nils suggested, "We will have to decide when we want to sign out of the hotel. I'm supposed to be at work Monday morning; but if we have to load the posters at four in the morning, I'm wondering if I should call the office and extend my holiday with you?"

"I'm scheduled to return home Tuesday morning, which will work perfectly as I want to travel aboard the *Ladybug* when it leaves Malmo early Monday morning for Copenhagen. That will give me more time to visit with Captain Oscarson and a full day to see the sights in Denmark." Seth brightened with the thought, "Nils, why don't you come to Denmark with me. We can both act like tourists and have some fun."

"That sounds like a plan to me." Nils quickly affirmed. "With this espionage thing going on, we haven't had time to just hang out."

With a furrowed brow, Seth advised, "I think we should check out late this afternoon. I don't want to have to carry that expensive Kosta lead crystal vase with me all day around Malmo."

Their conversation ended quickly when the wall clock chimed the noon hour. Both men jumped to their feet regretting they had lost track of time and would be late for their meeting with Fritz and Karl at The Flea Market. It was only a few blocks away, but they knew they would have to hurry.

The lobby was void of all tourist groups with only a few people gathered at the receptionist's desk, and two people sat at a table in a secluded corner playing solitaire… it was the odd couple.

Seth surmised, "I think they dress in the same identifying clothes so we will notice them," and questioned, "Are we becoming paranoid in thinking they are stalking us?"

The two looked at one another in disbelief and with a puzzled thought, Nills replied, "If they aren't, then it's sure coincidental they appear wherever we are. It's like we see them and then we don't… they just vanish."

Jokingly, Nils scrunched his face in a menacing expression, lowered his voice to sound like Dracula, and hoarsely muttered, "Things are getting too spooky!"

Both men laughed at their silly assumption; but half believing their theory, darted out the hotel lobby and scurried into the streets where they could get lost in a sea of tourists. The Malmo Festival is extremely popular and with the added attraction of the Tall Ships in the harbor, crowds of people from many countries were swarming all over the city. They took a circuitous route to the Flea Market, glancing back many times taking precaution they were not followed. It was difficult to weave through the curious tourists as they pushed and shoved to get the best advantage spot to purchase items from the many small booths lining the streets displaying merchandise. They regretted there was no designated street where they were to meet, but decided to wait for them underneath the Swedish flags and rested against the wall of the old well when Fritz and Karl approached.

Fritz was livid! In the heat of his frustration with glaring, penetrating eyes and red hot words rolling off his tongue, he yelled, "Where in the hell have you two been? Karl and I have circled this Flea Market several times looking for you."

In feverish excitement, Seth and Nils turned swiftly skimming the multitude of people in the street to determine if anyone within earshot were listening.

Fritz still wanted to vent his anger and while looking at Nils snarled, "Then, I remembered you could never get out of bed for an early morning class in college." Fritz soothed his frustration, but Nils became adamant wanting to lash back when Seth put his arm on Nils' shoulder to keep him quiet. Seth looked at Fritz with a stern expression and whispered, "If this is supposed to be a secret meeting, you just blew it!"

Karl suggested they walk to appear as tourists and the four slowly mingled with the crowd.

In a calm, informative manner, Seth continued while strolling by the booths, "Well, this *is* the Malmo Festival and Nils and I had a little fun after you dropped us off at the hotel. It was quite late last night, or I should say it was early this morning when we got to bed."

Seth's whole demeanor changed to an expression of happiness and reported, "I have some great…."

Fritz interrupted blasting forth, "You mean this morning you forgot about the serious business of safely transporting our blueprints to Copenhagen. Good heavens, man! Lives could be at stake in our attempt to do this." His voice becomes high-pitched as he continues, "My uncle's apartment was ransacked late yesterday afternoon after we left. The robbers were brave to attempt a robbery when my aunt was home alone; but thankfully, she was not hurt. They were violent in their destruction… as if a tornado had ripped through the rooms."

Seth, Nils and Karl remained quiet and urged Fritz to lower his voice. Fritz regained his composure and cheerfully informed, "After the four of us left the apartment late yesterday afternoon, my uncle, aunt and their two sons placed the blueprints behind the posters, affixed the frames for security and leaned them against the wall. The posters were not even moved." Fritz breathed a sigh of relief.

Seth eagerly asked, "Where are the posters, now?"

Karl was quick to answer, "The truck picked them up at ten this morning and I rode in the back of the truck to make sure they would arrive safely at the performance stage for musicians in Malmo. Fritz and his uncle drove behind the truck and all the band members arrived on time. The posters have been placed on the stage and the band is setting up the sound system for the performance this evening." With a worried thought, Karl mentioned, "The thieves only have today and tomorrow to steal the blueprints. After the concert is over in Tivoli Gardens, we have asked for police protection to deliver the posters to our lawyer's office and beyond to the government patent office in Copenhagen."

Once again, in a high-pitched voice filled with apprehension, Fritz pleaded, "How in the hell are we going to get the posters to Copenhagen after the performance tonight?"

Seth beamed with happiness and was ready to divulge his plan of action for transporting the blueprints when Karl urged everyone to sit down at an outside café where they could discuss the problem in a confined area where no tourists could hear their conversation. The waitress was quick to ask for their order while Fritz and Karl did not take a breath between hurriedly suggesting ideas... all of which failed miserably for a successful plan. Both flailed their arms in total frustration when they ran out of ideas and rested their arms on the table.

Seth and Nils looked at one another during the hectic discourse when Seth interrupted by resting his hands on their arms as if to harness the motion and quietly volunteered, "I have the perfect plan."

Fritz and Karl stared at Seth in disbelief and both voiced the same question, "What?"

With alacrity, Seth told the story of meeting a good friend, Captain Oscarson, master of the tramp steamer *Ladybug* at the wharf last night and enthusiastically reported the captain is willing to transport the posters to Copenhagen as a favor. He emphasized the importance of having the posters at the dock before four in the morning, as the ship has to be out of the harbor to accommodate the race of the Tall Ships.

The good news overwhelmed Fritz and Karl. They tried to quell the urge for a victory yell by expressing a euphoric gesture of thanks by slapping Seth on the back... and Karl enthusiastically questioned, "Why didn't you tell us immediately?"

Seth good-naturedly injected, "You two were throwing wild ideas around so fast, I couldn't break into your brain-power thinking."

"Hell, man, you've solved our problem!" Fritz became condescending with gratefulness and quietly reprimanded his own actions and words vehemently spoken for their tardiness to meet him and Karl at the Flea Market. "I want to apologize for taking you to task for not fully understanding the importance of our mission," and he felt the need to explain, "Our architectural firm is counting on us to deliver the blueprints. The scope of this project is immense and it could establish our company as one of the best in the world."

The four men sat quietly for quite awhile absorbing the good news... not wanting to break the euphoric spell.

After the waitress took an order for another round of drinks, Seth broke the silence when his thoughts spurred him to divulge the story of how he met Captain Oscarson. In a tone of voice charged with a nostalgic lilt, he reminisced about his journey aboard the *Ladybug* from Le Havre, France to Hong Kong, China. He told the story with passion believing Captain Oscarson was his mentor and father figure during the voyage... and was the driving force at that time in his life, which helped him grow to become a man in wisdom of worldly matters.

The three men could easily see Seth held this man in high esteem as he continued to explain the captain is an academic, literally a walking encyclopedia of knowledge, gentle and kind, but with a bellicose disposition when required to command his men aboard the tramp steamer, *Ladybug*. Seth murmured: "It has been a gratifying friendship."

He closed his eyes as his thoughts conjured up his favorite memory of the *Ladybug* ... the first time he saw Rachel. He could visualize the scene: she was standing on a small sampan, which had pulled close to the *Ladybug* in Victoria Harbor. The morning sunlight captured the beauty of her face and he knew it was love at first sight. Love for Rachel tightened his throat and choked his voice... and he remained quietly with a dejected feeling. He could not muster the desire to continue the story of Captain Oscarson.

By now, Nils can recognize the expression on Seth's face when he is thinking about Rachel and suggests, "I think we should tell them about the odd couple."

Karl energetically asks, "What's this? What about the odd couple?"

"Either we are becoming paranoid, or this strange man and woman are in fact scoping out our every move. To refresh your memory: we first noticed them on the bus to Christinehof to see Fritz; we saw them again at the hotel where they have reservations; and if you recall, they were in Lund to hear Seth's lecture. Well, we saw them late last night at the wharf when we talked to Captain Oscarson; and we saw them again in the hotel lobby this morning," and with an added thought, "Who knows where they are now."

"Fritz, you didn't tell me you saw the odd couple at Christinehof!" Karl implored.

"I noticed them, because they took the tour three consecutive days, which I thought was strange; and after we left Lund, if you remember the three of us went to the hotel where we found out they are traveling on an Italian passport and are owners of a fashionable lady's boutique in Milan. Since then, I have not considered them a threat, but I didn't know they keep popping up everywhere."

The four sat at the table watching the tourists meander from one booth to another looking to purchase the perfect treasure from Sweden. They sat back in their chair relaxing for only a few minutes… thankful their problem to transport the blueprints to Copenhagen had been solved. The joy was short-lived however, for now looming before them is an enlarged shadow of impending danger of keeping the posters safe before the transfer can be made from the stage to the ship. The musicians will perform on stage until two in the morning, which provides many hours where something can go wrong.

To exacerbate the situation, storm clouds are expected to roll in sometime in the early evening hours. The severity of the storm may preclude the process for safely transferring the posters to the ship. If the storm continues into Monday morning, the *Ladybug* will not be able to leave the harbor as scheduled and the Tall Ships' race will have to be postponed. Right now, everything is contingent on the weather and no precautionary plans can be made. The posters have to remain on the stage until, or if, the concert is canceled because of bad weather. It will be a wait-and-see game.

The sky was overcast with grey, ominous clouds and the four agreed they must have a temporary plan of action. They decided each man will stake out his territory for constant surveillance within sight of the stage for any suspicious movement within the area. Karl will rent the truck on stand-by basis for picking up the posters at the stage for transfer to the ship by two-thirty… or earlier if required. Fritz will report the good news that Seth has solicited help from his friend Captain Oscarson to transport the posters to Copenhagen; and the uncle will help to set up the sound equipment on the stage.

Seth and Nils advised they must return to the hotel to check out before four o'clock in the afternoon; they will take their luggage to the ship for safe keeping, and will return to the stage area to continue their surveillance.

Fritz urged everyone to be vigilant and cautious in monitoring the crowd as they do not know who or how many thieving corporate pirates are involved.   The four men felt confident they had discussed every angle of concern and left the café to assume their responsibilities.

Chapter Ten

The last day of the Malmo Festival, is always an exciting day when most guests will leave the hotel very early in the morning and return late at night. The festival was well organized leaving the tourists with a full day's schedule of events to enjoy. The lobby was void of any activity with only the receptionist and bellhop speaking softly at the desk.

———

Two men worked silently and swiftly in a hotel room... once again ripping clothes from suitcases, pulling mattresses from beds, going through dresser drawers and closets, and removing pictures from walls. They found nothing. An occasional nervous, dry cough was the only sound breaking the silence. They are masters in the profession of espionage where danger is always involved, and they have managed to elude exposing their identity. They are craftsmen of their trade.

Disgruntled and spewing obscenities, the men completely trashed the room, leaving a large blue duffel bag rumpled on the floor with an expensive Kosta crystal vase conspicuously safe on the night stand next to the bed. They know they are running out of options and time to look for the blueprints and their anxiety to complete this job is forcing them to take chances. This is their second visit to Room

43 on the fourth floor. After the unsuccessful search of the uncle's apartment and now again an unsuccessful search of Seth's and Nils' hotel room, they can only assume the blueprints are still in the uncle's possession.

They were not satisfied with the hostile raid on the uncle's apartment, having to abort their search too quickly. They took a few minutes to visualize the rooms and in retrospect the two realized the only things they did not check were the posters that were leaning against the wall. With a surprised look of realization, they both had the same thought: *Could it be the blueprints are behind the posters?*

They remembered the posters advertise the band's concerts in Malmo and in Copenhagen and the tour guide enthusiastically informed, "That's it! What a perfect place to hide the blueprints. The band is playing in Copenhagen tomorrow and the blueprints have to be delivered to the lawyer's office for transfer to the patent office in Copenhagen."

Smiling with a brilliant idea, the accomplice was quick to add, "We have certainly looked everywhere else. That has to be the hiding place!"

The men silently closed the door behind them; glanced down the long hallway for safety clearance, and walked toward the elevator. The elevator door opened to permit them to enter, but first they had to allow a man and woman to step out. With a startled expression, the tour guide lowered his eyes and bowed his head hoping not to be recognized. He wondered: *has another architectural firm hired this odd couple to steal the blueprints?*

The odd couple waited for the elevator door to close before quickly and silently walking down the hall to Room 43. They cautiously turned the door knob to see if the door was locked, and were surprised when the door opened to a room that had been thoroughly trashed. They scurried farther down the hallway to their room and closed the door.

Simultaneously, a second elevator stopped on the fourth floor. Seth and Nils walked the short distance to Room 43, but before Nils could put the key in the lock, Seth nudged him to look down the hallway... both men watched as the odd couple entered their room.

Seth whispered, "I didn't know their room is on our floor."

There was no need for Nils to turn the key in the lock as the door was open and the two entered to see the room had been ransacked once again.

Nils uttered with tongue in cheek, "I'm getting tired of this messy room. I think we should check out, now." He looked around the room noticing the Kosta vase was sitting proudly on the night stand having survived the tornadic attack. Nils chuckled aloud, "I guess these corporate pirates appreciate expensive glass."

"Yes, well," Seth advised, "this means they are not out to steal valuable items. They are only interested in stealing the blueprints." He opined, "After they did not find them at the apartment, they probably thought we still have them in our possession."

"Nils asked, "Do you think the odd couple did this?"

"I don't know." Seth replied with a worried thought, "Thank goodness, the blueprints are safe."

———

The elevator door opened to the lobby and the tour guide and accomplice left the hotel unnoticed.

Chapter Eleven

A few days ago, two friends set out on a course to enjoy the sights and sounds of Sweden. Little did they know they would become embroiled in a dangerous espionage caper... one where their lives could be in jeopardy. They knew they had to work quickly gathering their belongings and straightening up the room so they could return to the concert stage to maintain vigilance for the safety of the posters. When they were satisfied their suitcases were packed and the Kosta glass vase was safely wrapped in bubble wrap in the duffle bag, they stopped at the door to take one more glance around the room.

Nils looked down at the duffle bag in wonderment, "If this vase could talk, it would have an exciting story to tell." Both men started to chuckle to relieve tension.

"I sure hope Rachel likes it. It's been a real pain lugging it everywhere in this big over-sized duffle bag." With a wishful thought, Seth continued, "It's too bad Fritz would not let me pick out something small, which would have fit easily into my suitcase, but then I could not have carried the blueprints to Karl. So I guess I'm stuck with this big bag... and the vase."

Seth suggested, "Nils, why don't you grab something at the snack bar while I make a phone call."

There was no one in the lobby; and after checking out at the receptionist desk, Seth placed a call to his dad. "Hey, dad, how are you?"

"Hi, son, I've been waiting for your call. How did the lecture go?"

Seth was enthusiastic when he reported on the lecture at Lund University, but the tone of his voice changed dramatically to a sense of urgency when he asked, "Did Rachel call?"

"Yes," BillyJoe replied but was interrupted with a quick question.

"Is she coming home?" Seth was eager to hear the answer.

With a drawn-out, "Well," BillyJoe quietly reported, "she may stay in China for awhile. She said the people are having problems adjusting to Mao Tse-tung's party with the Great Leap Forward plan... which is proving to be greatly exaggerated." He thought for a moment remembering the conversation and continued, "There is a shortage of food; natural disasters including a tsunami in the Shanghai area; there is no one who can manage industry so it is floundering; Mao's political ideals are fragile; and it seems the whole idea for his plan is heading for economic failure. The students and workers are becoming restless with a feeling of betrayal. Rachel thinks it could possibly lead to a revolt."

Seth asked, "How are conditions on the Island of Lantau? Are the Chinese people feeling any repercussion there? Or... really, how are Rachel and the orphanage?"

BillyJoe reported, "Rachel said the children are leaving the big cities by droves in search of food and asylum, and the word has spread quickly the orphanage is a safe refuge. Three of the four dormitories are already filled to capacity and they are in desperate need of teachers. The monks from the Po Lin Monastery are generous beyond belief supplying the orphanage with milk, and the poor peasants share what clothing they can spare with the orphans."

Seth surmised, "The situation sounds as dire as it was shortly after World War II when Rachel's dad built the orphanage."

BillyJoe encouragingly volunteered, "This is a monstrous undertaking; and if there is anyone who can manage it successfully, it is General von Horstmann. I read an article in one of the magazines that her dad has curtailed drug smuggling in the Hong Kong-Canton area by seventy percent. The general is a brilliant strategist."

Seth agreed, "Yes, I know. That is just one of the reasons why Rachel idealizes her father," and with a discouraged thought: *and I have to compete with him for her love.*

Seth asked, "Did Rachel ask anything about me?"

In a quiet murmur BillyJoe answered, "She started to cry when I mentioned I had not heard from you because of the time difference between here and Sweden. I waited a few seconds for her to say something, but she just said 'good-bye' and we hung up."

Seth was too depressed to tell his dad about the espionage plot and his involvement in helping to secure the delivery of the Oresund Bridge blueprints to Copenhagen. His thoughts dwelled on Rachel and with a hurried "so long" the two ended the phone call.

The word tsunami triggered Seth to remember Rachel's and his harrowing experience of surviving one in Yokohama, Japan where she was held captive for ransom by drug traffickers. Her capture was even more dangerous when compounded with a tsunami. He shook his head in disbelief that their abiding love for one another was nourished from many devastating experiences. He ached to the pit of his stomach to hold her in his arms... to feel the warmth of her curvaceous body. The desire was so strong he closed his eyes trying to wipe out the memory of that last terrible argument.

Seth sat in the hotel lobby by the telephone for quite awhile with maudlin thoughts consuming his lifeless spirit when Nils returned from the snack bar with a puzzled look on his face, "You were thinking about your wife again, weren't you?"

A low moan whispered from his lips, "Yes."

"Is it healthy to love a woman that much? You look terrible." Nils shook his head wondering, "I was thinking of proposing to my girl next weekend, but you're not setting a very good example for married life."

Seth did not dignify Nils' stupid question with an answer, but urged, "Come on! Let's go! We have to take our suitcases to the *Ladybug.* I bet Fritz is already worried, wondering what is taking us so long to check out of the hotel."

Chapter Twelve

It was no easy chore to carry luggage and a huge duffel bag through the crowded streets of the Malmo Festival. Tourists were in a frenzy to take in all the sights and events before the dark clouds emptied their full supply of rain. The duffel bag was nudged and jostled by the pedestrians as Seth worked his way toward the harbor, and more than once he thought about giving the vase to a tourist. His desire to be free of the vase and the duffel bag ended when he remembered how expensive they are. His thoughts rambled: *it's no longer a beautiful lead crystal Kosta vase... it's the damn vase!* And he continued plodding along protecting the duffel bag.

Captain Oscarson was standing on the deck of the *Ladybug* looking toward the horizon with the billowing dark clouds rolling into the area.

With a hearty "hello" and a smile, he called, "Step aboard, gentlemen. I've been waiting for you. What are your plans?"

Seth and Nils returned his greeting with a handshake as they stepped onto the deck. The three slowly walked to the bow of the ship where they could talk without being heard by the deckhands. Both men took turns telling the captain about the corporate pirates' vicious invasions of the uncle's apartment and twice in their hotel room.

Seth brightened when he reported on their noon meeting with Fritz and Karl. "They both express their thanks to you for offering the ship to transport the posters to Copenhagen," and he   explained further, "The posters are on the stage now where they will remain until after the concert tonight when they will be delivered to the ship."

All three looked up at the swirling clouds. The storm is coming in from the west and Captain Oscarson knows he cannot set sail for Copenhagen now or even tonight as the ship is currently locked into the harbor by the Tall Ships. All ship movement will depend upon the weather as to when or if the ships can leave the harbor on schedule.

"Our last weather report stated the storm will hit Malmo this evening about eight o'clock; and if that is the case, then I'm certain the concert will be canceled and the posters can be brought to the ship shortly thereafter. The ship will not move, however, until we receive clearance to do so." Captain Oscarson volunteered and suggested, "Why don't you two put your luggage in one of the rooms below. Seth, I'm sure you will remember the way."

Seth directed Nils to the cabins below deck, noticing nothing had changed on the ship. It was as if time had stopped. He remembered everything as he led Nils down the dark hallway. He selected the same room where he stayed for many weeks when he traveled aboard the *Ladybug* from Le Harve to Hong Kong. It was a nostalgic moment of memories, which will last his lifetime.

The two men placed their luggage in the rooms and returned to the top deck to witness Captain Oscarson directing one of his deckhands in the proper placement of ropes.

"I don't want any obstacles on deck, which may hamper a speedy loading of the posters tonight." Captain Oscarson turned to look at the deckhand as he tended to his duties and discouragingly reported to Seth, "Good seamen are still hard to find... some aren't worth their salt."

"Captain," Seth reported, "Nils and I will be at the concert tonight throughout the whole performance in surveillance of the crowd for any suspicious movement. We do not know the identity of the corporate pirates for certain, but we think there are at least four people who need watching. I will get word to you if the concert is canceled. If by luck the storm does not come to Malmo and the band can play until two in the morning, then the truck will deliver the posters to the ship by two-thirty, which will be in good time for you to clear the harbor by four as you request."

With a fatherly touch on Seth's shoulder, Captain Oscarson cautioned, "Be extremely careful. The corporate pirates know who you are, but you are not certain of their identity. There may be more of them than you think."

Seth and Nils started to walk down the gangplank when Captain Oscarson called, "Seth, holdup! Wait a minute."

Both returned to the deck

With a perplexing thought the captain continued, "You mentioned your hotel room was trashed; the uncle's apartment was ransacked; and then once again the pirates trashed your room."

Seth stopped the captain, "Yes, that's right!"

"I believe the pirates' logical thinking would be to reconsider that the blueprints are still at the uncle's apartment, as their invasion was aborted before they had a chance to search everywhere thoroughly." The captain scratched the back of his head and suggested, "I think it stands to reason they will want to look closer at the posters."

Seth shook his head in agreement, "Yes, they may remember they didn't even move the posters, which were leaning against the wall undisturbed."

"I think you should hide the blueprints in your big duffel bag again… and make the transfer as quickly as possible." The captain looked at Nils for agreement.

Nils was quick to add, "Yes, I agree."

Seth thought out loud, "The pirates know we have to get the blueprints to Copenhagen to register them at the patent office; and since they have not been successful thus far in locating them, they may figure the posters are the ideal hiding place."

Without saying another word, Seth left the deck to return to his cabin below. He removed the damn vase from the duffel bag; left it in the bubble wrap and placed it gently on the bed. He grabbed the empty duffel bag and returned to the top deck.

Both men left the ship and scurried through the crowd at the harbor, forcing their way to the concert stage area. They were anxious to talk to Fritz.

———

Fritz yelled, "Where in the hell have you two been!" His face was red with rage. "I have never seen such lackluster vigilance in the performance of duty. I don't know how else to explain it to you that this is a very serious undertaking... we need all the help we can..."

Seth did not appreciate being scolded when Fritz did not understand the whole situation of events that had taken place in the last couple of hours. "Stop right there!" Seth was adamant, "Let Nils and me tell you what has happened!"

It was evident Fritz was losing patience with his two friends. The pressure was building within him to a point where his instinctive inclination to criticize severely was taking over the necessity for caution. A new factor, the weather, is now a crucial concern to be considered for a successful transfer of the blueprints... and Fritz feels overwhelmed.

Karl and the uncle heard Fritz from a distance and once again advised that he lower his voice. The five men walked slowly, trying to be as inconspicuous as possible, to an area behind the stage where the rental truck was parked.

The three men listened attentively as Seth and Nils divulged the incidents which caused their delay in returning to the stage. It was more than a briefing as they spoke at great length clearly giving a full report.

A brilliant light zigzagged across the sky followed by a roll of thunder rumbling through the dark clouds causing some tourists to scramble for shelter, while a larger percentage of music enthusiasts were going to remain vigil at the stage... or at least until the rain came down in torrents. The band members were on stage playing the first set of songs and, per their contract, would continue to play until the rain would chase them off the stage. The posters were in full view providing an attractive backdrop for the band.

The uncle speculated, "If Captain Oscarson's theory is correct, that the pirates will try to confiscate the posters... subsequently, I think his suggestion is correct. We should remove the blueprints and transfer them to Copenhagen in the duffel bag."

Fritz loudly reminded him, "Uncle, they are on the stage!"

"Calm down! Now listen," the uncle continued, "My wife insisted we place a clear plastic cover over the posters to protect them from any damage to the surface of the painting while in transport by truck to the stage. Let's remove one poster at a time from the stage before it starts to rain; work in the truck with the door closed; remove the blueprints, put the plastic cover over the front and return it to the stage. The audience will think we are taking justifiable precaution for these posters," and to praise his wife's artistic ability, "they are really a work of art."

Fritz breathed a sigh of relief, suggesting, "Uncle, I think you and I should work in the truck. Karl can stand by the stage to assist with moving the posters on and off, and Seth and Nils can mingle with the crowd at the front of the stage to watch for any suspicious actions."

Nils was quick to inject, "Sounds like a good plan to me." Nils nudged the duffel bag, which was placed on the ground, with his shoe and cheerfully volunteered, "I know Seth will be happy to be rid of this damn thing."

"You haven't heard the best part of the plan, yet," the uncle declared with a big smile. "My sons and I were able to place all the blueprints behind one poster, but backed all four of them with plywood and secured them with a large frame so they would all be identical in construction."

For the first time in quite awhile, Fritz' worried frown changed to a happy expression and with a wide grin said, "That's great, uncle! I think we have a good plan. The corporate pirates will think the blueprints are behind the posters; and I assume they will try to confiscate them somewhere between here and the *Ladybug.*" To lay out the plan further, Fritz continued, "Karl and I will take the blueprints in the duffel bag with us on the ferryboat to Copenhagen."

The uncle placed his arm on Fritz' shoulder for encouragement, bowed his head in reverence and quietly suggested, "Let's all pray the velocity of the storm will not hit Malmo's harbor area with full force. I have seen gigantic waves on the Oresund Strait where no ship could safely sail for days. The *Ladybug* and the Tall Ships will have to remain in the harbor for safety and the sailing schedule will depend upon the weather." With an added thought, the uncle remembered, "And the small ferryboat will have to be safe also from the storm so it can keep its regularly scheduled departures from Malmo over the Oresund Strait to Copenhagen and return." The uncle looked at Fritz and Karl suggesting, "Your trip across the Strait may be delayed for awhile. We will have to be flexible and adjust our plans accordingly."

Fritz was quick to respond, "Uncle, you just made an excellent argument for building this bridge over the Oresund Strait. We can use this storm in our publicity campaign to express beyond a doubt the necessity to connect the two countries." With great pride, Fritz burst forth, "and we have the best set of plans in our possession, which when a suspension bridge, an island, and a tunnel are all constructed, it will be a miraculous feat of engineering the world has yet to see."

Upon hearing Fritz' remark, the tension eased among the other men as if it were a pep talk to rally their spirits with renewed vitality to protect the blueprints and to deliver them to the proper authorities.

Each man performed his task with revived energy. The uncle selected the poster bearing the blueprints to be removed first from the stage to the truck... where they were safely transferred to the large duffel bag. With Karl's assistance, Fritz and the uncle worked skillfully taking one poster at a time to the truck where the clear plastic cover was placed over them.

There was no disturbance to the band's performance as the audience assumed that because of the slight mist in the air, the task was necessary and gave no further thought to the quiet interruption. Many partying revelers gathered close to the stage to dance to the music as the band's magical sound produced a merrymaking environment.

After their work was done, Fritz and Karl each picked up an instrument case from the truck, a small duffel bag filled with sheets of music, which items were used as decoys if someone were watching, and the large blue duffel bag containing the blueprints. They placed everything in the trunk of Fritz' car and drove to the uncle's apartment.

Seth and Nils each went their separate way in the crowd, enjoying the music while looking for familiar faces... the odd couple and the tour guide.

Chapter Thirteen

A rather large moving van pulled onto a side street adjacent to the festival area behind the concert stage. The driver slowly and cautiously proceeded to back into an open area to park when a policeman approached, calling to the driver, "Hey, buddy, you're going to have to move your van out of this area."

The driver rolled down the window, coughed a few times while pointing to a truck already parked directly behind the stage and in an angry tone of voice asked, "How come that truck can be there and I can't park my van here? I'm a block away!"

The policeman was becoming a little agitated and firmly stated, "You see that big permit on the windshield... that's how come it can park there... and for the duration of the festival. Now, get moving!"

Trying to talk through a nervous cough, the driver curtly advised, "Those guys in the band asked me to help them move their sound equipment and the posters tonight, and they agreed to pay me a healthy sum of money... and I need the cash! And you're telling me I can't park here!"

The policeman realized the situation could escalate into an ugly scene and decided to help the driver solve his problem and suggested, "Alright! Get out and go ask them what they want you to do."

Not wanting to draw attention from the band, the driver quickly responded, "I'm going to forget it and chalk it up to a lesson learned."

Both men glared at one another with nothing being said. The driver mumbled a few expletives under his breath, coughed a few times, and moved the van.

The policeman stood his ground for several minutes, making certain the van would leave the area; and when it was out of sight, he continued to patrol the festival grounds for any unlawful incidents. The last day of the festival is historically the most raucous and he was prepared to handle anything that would come his way. He had walked only a short distance when a couple of tourists stopped him. The man wore a sweatshirt with Stockholm printed on the front and the woman wore a blue and yellow hat with Stockholm printed on the brim.

The man curiously asked, "Why was he so upset? I thought we were going to witness a fight."

"Naw, he was upset because he wasn't going to get paid a large sum of money for helping the band members move their equipment and posters after the performance. But from the looks of the sky, they may have to move sooner than later. Maybe, he should have circled the block a few times."

The odd couple laughed, "Well a good paying job is hard to find," and continued walking.

The uncle also witnessed the confrontation between the driver and the policeman from the stage backdoor. He was certain the driver, who constantly coughed, was the thief who broke into his apartment and he wondered if the tourists, who match the identity given to him by Seth and Nils, were the odd couple. He knew everyone would have to be vigilant expecting the possibility there may be other corporate pirates. He maintained his position at the stage backdoor for quite some time... always looking for the van to return.

The policeman continued to circle the stage area on a regular schedule for any mischief-makers, but the crowd was dwindling in size and in enthusiasm as the storm clouds rolled with thunder.

When Fritz and Karl arrived at the uncle's apartment, they were greeted by the aunt, who immediately directed them downstairs to a secluded closet in the basement. The closet door was well hidden behind a large bookcase, which sat directly on the floor, but rested on low rollers for easy moving. They placed the large duffel bag bearing the blueprints in the closet feeling satisfied it was a safe hiding place.

The two men wasted no time in returning to the festival and reported to the uncle, "Our worries are over for the time being. The blueprints are safe in your security closet in the basement."

"Yes," the uncle acknowledged, "I made that closet shortly after we moved into the apartment. It's not a first-class neighborhood, but it's all I can afford, right now. I like the assurance that things are safe there."

The band continued to play popular songs with a musical beat, which inspired the crowd to dance and sing. At times, it was difficult to hear the rumble of the thunder while the loud speakers blasted away with the chromatic sounds of jazz making conversation almost impossible. Eight, nine, ten o'clock passed with only an occasional mist falling on the revelers; but at eleven, the clouds opened to release a torrent of rain and wind. Pushing and shoving in a chaotic effort, everyone scrambled to seek shelter. Quickly, the people turned into a massive, moving force like a herd of buffalo racing across the plains. There was no friendliness nor civility as the frenzied horde turned on one another lashing out with fists... and a spontaneous, ugly fistfight ensued.

In the center of the brawl was the tour guide, who initiated the fight, throwing the first and second punch. That's all it took to get some of the drunken revelers involved, and within minutes there was a full-scale fight. Policemen came running from all directions around the concert stage to control the mob. Rain fell at an oblique angle urged by the force of the wind, but the men involved appeared to enjoy the fight too much to quit.

The tour guide bent low, squeezing through the fighting crowd, violently striking anyone in his way... and escaped, running as fast as he could to a van parked a short distance from the area. The odd couple did not join in the fight, but stood quietly and watched. When the tour guide forced his way clear of the melee, the couple was quick to follow.

Seth and Nils jumped onto the stage to help move the large posters to the truck, which was their first concern, while band members cased their instruments and worked to remove the sound equipment. Fritz, Karl and the uncle remained at the back stage door guarding the truck.

The slow-moving storm continued in all its fury blowing debris and anything that was not anchored down across the festival grounds. Merchants worked quickly to remove their craft items and tents, while tourists sought sanction from the heavy rain in nearby restaurants or in covered doorways. A long streak of lightening cracked across the sky followed by an ominous sound of thunder when a huge burst of fire with cascading sparks appeared at the site of the electric generators, which had been temporarily installed for the convenience of the crafters. Hot wires bounced across the ground producing an eerie design of light in the pitch-black festival area. The shrill sound of sirens could be heard in the distance as the fire trucks rushed to put out the fire. It was a frantic scene.

The men who were engaged in the fistfight dispersed into all directions, but the odd couple noticed there were a few men who hid in the darkness behind the stage watching Fritz and Karl loading the last of the four posters. The sound equipment would be the last to carry to the truck as the six band members worked feverishly and cautiously in the darkness with wet fingers that felt like all thumbs on the electric cords. Finally, the uncle remembered there was a flashlight in the glove pocket of the dashboard and flashed the light onto the sound equipment... the band members breathed a sigh of relief and quickly loaded everything into the truck.

As if the weather switch had been turned off, the force of the wind and the driving rain subsided as the tour guide ran to his van, which was a short distance away, but in view of the truck at the stage. The plan was to move the van behind the truck to block it from moving. With the aid of three accomplices, he felt confident with a surprise attack they could overpower the uncle and the four young men and transfer the posters to the van.

In reckless haste, the tour guide hopped into the van, hit the gas peddle; rolled and bounced twenty feet. He slammed on the brakes and flew out the door spewing expletives only a drunken sailor would understand, and walked around the van viciously kicking each of the four tires which had been slashed. He was beyond adamant... livid with rage. He had carefully planned this heist and could not understand what had happened. He flopped down in the cab of the van; bowed his head and closed his eyes feeling depressed and discouraged with no driving spirit to move him. This was the only chance he would have to confiscate the posters with the blueprints... and he had failed.

The roar of a motor aroused him to face the present situation. He was alert enough to see that Karl sat behind the wheel while Seth and Nils got into the truck. The tour guide watched as it slowly pulled away from the stage, thinking: *my dreams of selling the blueprints to a competitive architectural company have just slipped away.* He continued to watch the uncle and Fritz drive away. When the six band members left the stage, he realized his plan to steal the posters would have been more difficult than he thought as there would have been a total of eleven men involved against him and his three accomplices. Even with the element of surprise, the plan would have failed.

The odd couple wanted to shout with joy; but instead, they expressed their euphoric feeling silently with a very broad grin.

Chapter Fourteen

By the time the truck had arrived at the *Ladybug*, both the wind and the rain had stopped. There was debris scattered all over the wharf mostly from trash barrels, which had been filled to capacity by the festival revelers. Strong waves no longer crashed against the harbor wall, while the Tall Ships rested at anchor on the water having survived the storm. It was one o'clock in the morning when Karl, Seth and Nils arrived at the gangplank to unload the posters to the ship. The seaman on watch quickly left the deck to alert the captain.

Captain Oscarson cheerfully came on deck, calling to the three men as they walked up the gangplank, "For a slow moving storm, it carried a terrific wallop, but, thankfully, it was short-lived."

Seth joyfully exclaimed, "Are we happy to see you! I'll be glad when we unload the posters and have them safely aboard ship."

The captain was quick to ask, "Did you have any trouble?"

Karl answered, "No, and I don't know why not. There was a rather large moving van parked a short distance away, which we thought would be the vehicle to be used in stealing the posters... and we were diligent in keeping our eyes on it the whole time." He paused with the puzzled thought, "I thought it moved briefly for a short distance, but I guess the heavy rain, which was pelting the ground at the time, played tricks on my eyes." And in a light-hearted tone opined, "I think we were lucky and can thank the storm that the thieves did not, or could not, steal the posters."

The captain volunteered, "I'll help you unload the posters and then we can sit a spell over a glass of vodka when you can tell me about the successful transfer of the blueprints from the posters to the duffel bag."

Karl politely responded, "Thank you for the invitation and I could use a glass of vodka right now, but I have to drive the truck to the uncle's apartment and return it to the rental agency in the morning." He continued explaining their plan, "The uncle will return the truck and Fritz and I will take the blueprints to Copenhagen by ferryboat."

The men quickly transferred the posters to the ship; and after reminiscing for a short time about the events of the last two days, they said their good-byes to Karl, breathing a sigh of relief for a job well done and watched as the truck pulled away.

Seth, Nils and the captain enjoyed talking while sipping vodka as the early morning hours passed with no one getting any sleep. They watched as the sun rose brilliantly in a clear blue sky... almost in a teasing fashion that yesterday's storm was the dark side of weather. The three raised their glasses to toast "good luck" after the authorities advised the *Ladybug* could leave for Copenhagen on schedule.

———

After several hot cups of coffee and a hearty breakfast, Captain Oscarson directed his deckhands to prepare the ship for leaving port and to set a course for Copenhagen. The Tall Ships had already maneuvered into position with their seamen actively scurrying on deck completing final preparations to continue their race to the next port. Seth and Nils felt the excitement of the sport vicariously as the *Ladybug* gracefully cut through the water at a close distance. The two men stood at the railing admiring the beautiful ships as they sailed for the open water of the Oresund Strait

Considering the late-night storm vented its fury wreaking havoc on the festival, the early morning weather was crisp with a spectacular sunrise and the two men lingered longer on deck watching the deckhands perform their duties. Nils was impressed with the energy level they expended and asked Seth what he knew about the life of a sailor on a tramp steamer.

Seth thought for a moment about his weeks spent on the *Ladybug* and in a pundit style replied, "The master of a tramp steamer will list his ports of call on a placard, which will be posted in the shipping office. The ship will sail to ports and places in any part of the world covering many seas as the master may direct, returning to the port of discharge for a term of time not to exceed twelve months. There are rules and regulations to be followed and the master will direct if or when a seaman may leave the ship to visit a port of call." Seth stopped to admire the seamen and continued, "Sailing to ports of call all over the world may be a romantic and an exciting dream, but it is a lot of hard work with long hours."

Nils gave the commentary deep thought and volunteered, "The idea of a romantic, exciting adventure while seeing the world appeals... but I would not like the hard work and I definitely would not like the long hours." In a slow whisper, he added, "I think I'll stick to being an architect."

———

Activity at the Malmo city wharf was exceptionally busy with spectators eagerly jostling one another for the best position to view the parade of the beautiful Tall Ships as they passed into the open water. The *Ladybug* also sailed by the spectators and Seth and Nils joined in the festivity by waiving to the crowd.

The ferryboat schedule was reinstated immediately after the weather bureau gave the okay to transport passengers across the Oresund Strait. Fritz and Karl made plans accordingly to catch the first boat from Malmo to Copenhagen and stood in a long line at the ticket office, as did many tourists who had the same idea, hoping to catch their flights home from the Copenhagen airport.

The two men were among the first to board the ferryboat and chose seats next to the exit door where they would be first to disembark in Copenhagen. Fritz took an aisle seat and placed the blue duffel bag on an adjoining seat next to Karl. With a feeling it was tightly secured between the two of them, he breathed a sigh of relief that this dangerous episode in his life would be over, soon. The previous few days were more than difficult... he agonized through every hour with a heavy feeling of worry. The two men sat quietly... watching the tourists take their seats when Fritz was nudged rather forcefully on the shoulder by a tourist walking in the aisle. He looked up with a startled expression. It was the tour guide.

"Good morning," the tour guide cheerfully said, "I remember you. You're the clerk from the gift shop at Christinehof and I see you have bought one of those large blue duffel bags." And continued, "That's the third one I've seen in the last few days."

He continued to focus his eyes on the duffle bag for a few seconds while nothing was said.

In frustration, Fritz managed a stilted smile, "Oh, yes, we've sold quite a few of them."

"I'd better grab a seat before they are all taken," the tour guide advised as he moved farther down the aisle.

Fritz and Karl remained quiet... not even looking at one another when suddenly everyone turned around to witness a noisy altercation between tourists regarding who was going to get the last two seats at the back of the boat. Fritz and Karl could not believe their eyes. The odd couple won the seats.

Fritz remembered when Seth mentioned he was becoming paranoid in thinking he and Nils were being followed by the odd couple... and the tour guide. He thought: *Could it be possible they are following Karl and me.* Fritz and Karl looked at one another... not saying a word, but their eyes said it all. First fear; then hope... that the tour guide and/or the odd couple were going to Copenhagen to meet the *Ladybug* when it docked to confiscate the posters.

Fritz smiled thinking: *They will be surprised to see the police waiting at the dock for the ship to arrive in order to provide an escort for the safe delivery of the posters to Tivoli Garden, which will make it appear that the posters still conceal the blueprints.*

With haggard faces and furrowed foreheads, the two men nervously wondered what would confront them when they arrive in Copenhagen.

Chapter Fifteen

The tour guide sat quietly in his seat at the bow of the ferryboat while the other passengers scrambled for their seats. His thoughts rambled to the afternoon at Christinehof when he shared a table at lunch with the gift-shop clerk, Fritz… and Seth and Nils. He dwelled upon the vision of the large duffel bag, which he surmised could easily hold a quantity of blueprints. He remembered when he and his accomplice searched Seth's hotel room the duffel bag contained a large crystal vase, and curiously thought: *Is it possible the vase was just a decoy, used at times to transfer the blueprints to the posters?*

He became frustrated, coughed more than usual, and nervously began cracking his knuckles, but stopped when the other passengers were annoyed by the sound and glared at him.

He was pleased with the plan to have his three accomplices stationed at the wharf waiting for the *Ladybug* to dock so they could steal the posters; and he felt confident they could handle any situation that may arise. He realized that his doubt that the blueprints are now in the duffel bag is a supposition, but thought: *perhaps it may be prudent that I should steal the duffel bag to be certain the blueprints are behind the posters.* With a smile on his face, he continued the thought: *if they are in the duffel bag, so much the better.* He worried that he would be up against two men, but with the added assurance afforded by a gun in his pocket, he thought he would be able to handle both of them.

Fritz and Karl thought it was a stroke of bad luck that the tour guide and the odd couple traveled with them to Copenhagen. They did not like the long, curious gaze the tour guide gave the duffel bag, as if trying to scrutinize its contents; and they never have been able to figure out the role the odd couple plays in transferring the blueprints to Copenhagen. They realized they would have to be alert and ready to react to any aggressive action by either the tour guide or the odd couple.

It was not a smooth ride on the ferryboat as the water continued to roll in waves blown by a brisk breeze from the tail end of the storm. The ferryboat would dock before the *Ladybug* at the wharf to allow the passengers to go ashore close to Copenhagen's city central.

Because of the storm, The *Ladybug* would be delayed in its arrival, as there was no birth immediately available at the wharf. It would have to drop anchor and remain in the harbor with other ships' awaiting sequential orders to move to the wharf to unload their cargo.

———

Time dragged slowly while the ferryboat ride seemed endless. Some did not like the rough ride on the choppy water caused by an occasional large wave and loudly voiced their discomfort, making the close environs of the nervous passengers electrically charged with fear for their safety. Even the captain's assurance that there was no real danger did not dispel their anxiety.

When the passengers saw the dock was a short distance away, most left their seats and started to push toward the exit door in a frenzied hurry to leave the boat. Regrettably, some were seasick. The scene was one of panic and Fritz and Karl decided it was best to let everyone leave the boat before they would attempt to leave carrying the large duffel bag. They noticed the tour guide and the odd couple had the same idea and they braced themselves for whatever would happen.

Since Fritz and Karl were seated close to the exit door, they waited for the opportune time to leave, quickly. Fritz grabbed the duffel bag and the two men walked the short gangplank with the tour guide forcibly pushing his way to get behind them... and the odd couple followed. When they stepped off the gangplank, Karl felt a gun at his back and called to Fritz: "Run! He's got a gun!"

The tour guide hit Karl on the head with the butt of his gun and he fell immediately. Fritz tried to run while carrying the large duffel bag through the crowded area, but the bag was definitely a hindrance and he was stopped by the disgruntled passengers who had left the ferryboat.

The tour guide grabbed Fritz' arm; held the gun at his back from under his coat when the odd couple pushed their way through the crowd and both the woman and man pounced upon the tour guide knocking him to the ground. They immediately took the gun and tied his hands behind his back. It all happened in a matter of seconds. Fritz stood paralyzed and dumfounded to what he had witnessed.

A large, curious crowd gathered... eager to find out what caused the excitement. Karl was a little dazed from the blow to his head, but pushed and stumbled into the center of the crowd. He was happy to see that Fritz had survived unscathed. The two men smiled at one another, feeling an emotion of thankfulness when they glanced at the large duffel bag safely beside them on the ground.

The odd couple continued to hold the tour guide until the harbor police arrived. It was obvious to Fritz and Karl that the man and woman were well trained as they competently handled the situation with ease.

When the harbor police arrived, Fritz stepped forward to talk, but was pushed aside by the odd couple, who produced identification and proceeded to explain what had happened. The story was completely fabricated having nothing whatsoever to do with posters or blueprints. The police were captivated by the story and suggested they would send a police car to escort Fritz and Karl to the lawyer's office in Copenhagen.

The four watched the police car drive away; turned and started laughing at the ridiculous story. It definitely helped ease the stress of the morning boat ride; and with a feeling of satisfaction for a job well done, the four slowly meandered to a nearby restaurant for lunch while they waited for a police escort.

Karl could not contain his anxiety any longer and asked, "Have you been on our side all along? We thought you were the bad guys!"

The man was quick to respond, "We were hired by your architectural firm to watch and protect you... and to always follow the blueprints."

Karl started to laugh, "How in the world did you ever manage to come up with that fairytale?" and repeated some of the story, "Fritz' dad's will and property deeds from Christinehof, and even his great, great grandfather's top hat and whatever else...?"

Fritz interrupted, "Well, it is a large duffel bag and he had to think of some things that would fill it...."

All four started to laugh. Karl surmised; shook his head and turned to Fritz, "It definitely helps when you have a respected, aristocratic name!"

The woman was next to report, "After you leave with the police escort, we will leave to await the arrival of the *Ladybug*. Our assignment will not be completed until Seth is safely aboard a plane to go home and Nils returns to Stockholm."

Fritz asked, "When you see Seth, will you please ask him to call me at the Mayfair Hotel in Copenhagen. I'd like to see him before he flies home."

Chapter Sixteen

The small run-down hotel across the boardwalk from the harbor was an ideal location for the three accomplices hired by the tour guide. They were in close proximity to the ships moored at the wharf and the Tall Ships anchored in the Oresund Strait. They were in constant surveillance of any movement aboard the *Ladybug*.

It was very early in the morning when the *Ladybug* received clearance from the port authorities to set sail; and as soon as the boat pulled away, the three men scurried to rent a speedboat. The agent at the rental office advised them they had to wait until the Tall Ships sailed out of the harbor before they could leave. This information was more than disconcerting as it was imperative they arrive in Copenhagen before the *Ladybug*.

The three joined the crowds of spectators who lined the harbor area. The atmosphere was quite festive with camera enthusiasts angling for the best view of the Tall Ships poised to begin the race, when they were vigorously jostled by a camera crew. Under any other circumstance, they would have retaliated or even picked a fight, but they had an expensive job awaiting them in Copenhagen and they did not want to lose the good money.

Finally, the ships were out of the harbor and the three men were given clearance to leave by speedboat. Literally, with caution to the wind, it was a frantic ride as the boat bounced from one large wave to another at great speed. Their tension relaxed when they saw the

Ladybug, and within a few minutes, the speedboat quickly moved ahead for a considerable distance. Their confidence was bolstered when they arrived in Copenhagen in good time to get to the truck rental office where the tour guide had previously reserved a large truck to be rented upon pickup.

———

The three accomplices were not happy when they sat in the truck in the cargo area at the Copenhagen dock. Because of the storm, all slips for cargo ships were currently occupied and they found out from the clerk in the harbor office, the *Ladybug* would not be permitted to enter a slip for a few hours. They were also concerned there were more harbor police in the area than they had ever seen. After awhile they found out the ferryboat had docked, and they were surprised the tour guide had not come to meet them as planned.

The three sat in the truck for four hours watching other cargo ships loading and unloading. With each passing hour, their dark thoughts created bad-tempered attitudes while discussing various devious reasons as to why the tour guide had not come. *Were they being set up to take the fall for the heist.*

They became very uncomfortable when they noticed city police had also joined the harbor police to patrol the area. They likened the scene to bees swarming around the hive and they hoped their truck would not be considered the center of the hive. The police became more inquisitive the longer they sat in the truck.

One of the harbor policemen approached the truck, "Hey, buddy, how long are you planning to sit here?"

The driver responded, "We are waiting for a ship to dock to help unload its cargo."

"What's the name of the ship?" The policeman pressured for an answer.

"I don't know. We were told a seaman would approach us if they needed extra help." The driver thought that was a good answer, but the policeman strictly advised, "You had better move along. Until all these ships unload, this is a restricted area for unauthorized personnel."

The driver asked, "What's with all the police in the area? Are you expecting trouble?"

"Just move along, buddy… now!" The policeman urged.

The truck slowly moved away carrying three men who were all cursing the tour guide at the same time. Red in the face with anger, and hitting their fists on the dashboard, each one took turns furiously expressing an idea of how to hurt the tour guide.

With a friendly wave of "thank you" to the policeman, the odd couple watched as the truck slowly left the area.

Chapter Seventeen

The short trip of ten miles crossing the Oresund Strait from Malmo, Sweden to Copenhagen, Denmark was not long enough for Seth to visit with his mentor, Captain Oscarson.

A stiff breeze continued to make an occasional large wave hit against the hull of the ship and   they were reminded of the voyage aboard the tramp steamer *Ladybug* when it sailed into the Pacific Ocean during a tropical storm after traversing the Panama Canal. That experience reinforced Seth's desire to find his "sea legs", and he did not get seasickness during the entire voyage. They shared many fond memories, which created a strong bond of friendship, teetering upon the two becoming surrogate father and son.

Nils could sense the respect they held for each other and silently wished he could relate to that feeling with his own father. With a forlorn thought, he bowed his head in deep contemplation rationalizing: *Perhaps, being the youngest of nine siblings makes the difference.* The experience learned during the last few days will be remembered for the rest of his life, as a special bond has been woven between him and Seth. Still in a somber mood, Nils regretted this dangerously fun episode was about to come to an end.

Seth enjoyed remembering the various events of his voyage from Le Harve, France to Hong Kong, China, even though some were life-threatening, but every memory of China discussed with the captain contained experiences shared with Rachel. He could not help becoming heavy hearted and extremely introspective of his reflective loving thoughts. A lump of passion came in his throat and he thought his heart would burst with love while lamenting, *Rachel, I miss you so much it hurts.*

Nils recognized Seth's sorrowful expression and knew he was thinking of Rachel. To divert the captain's attention, Nils asked, "After you leave Copenhagen, where is your next port?"

The captain was aware of Seth's quiet mood and answered with a cheerful, "I'm sailing to Morocco and I regret that you two young men can't sail with me. I think you would enjoy North Africa."

Nils and the captain carried on a long conversation, which made it quite evident to Nils that Captain Oscarson is definitely an intelligent man as Seth had said, "A walking encyclopedia".

After four hours bouncing in the Copenhagen harbor, the *Ladybug* was cleared to enter a birth at the wharf to have its cargo unloaded… and it moored late afternoon. The seamen were eager to complete this task. They worked at great speed, as Captain Oscarson promised the men they could enjoy the nightlife in Copenhagen… and going ashore was definitely one of the perks of being a sailor on a cargo ship. The many exciting foreign cities visited around the world provided these pleasure-seekers a variety in entertainment, making the hard work, mundane, and sometimes exciting life on the ship gainfully rewarding.

Captain Oscarson escorted the two young men to the gangplank, regretting once again, he would have to say good-bye to Seth. The two men clasped in a father/son hug. With suitcase in one hand and a large bubble-wrapped package in the other arm, Seth slowly walked down the gangplank. Nils followed behind, thanking the captain for his hospitality and hoping they would meet again some day.

They had walked a short distance, when Nils called, "Seth, look! It's the odd couple and they are walking toward us!"

Both men were flabbergasted and mumbled for the right words when they were approached.

With a pleasant expression and a smile on their face, the odd couple introduced themselves and unraveled a complex story of fiction leading to the truth of their purpose in being involved to watch and protect them. Seth and Nils attentively listened, but were still in a daze of disbelief, as the odd couple continued to inform them that Fritz and Karl had safely delivered the blueprints to the lawyer's office. They had many questions, which the odd couple were happy to answer and all four expressed their happiness for a successful end to a complicated assignment.

It was the sound of a large truck rumbling down the boardwalk that caught their attention. The truck stopped at the *Ladybug,* which was guarded by harbor patrol, and the band members hopped out to load the posters on the truck to deliver them to the concert stage in Tivoli Garden. The band members were happy to see Seth and Nils and questioned if they were going to come to their concert. With a cheerful answer, they both answered, "We'll be there!"

They all watched as the posters were loaded into the truck and expressed a sigh of relief. Each one had his own special memory of the difficult task to get the posters safely to Copenhagen. The band members thanked everyone for their assistance and drove away in the truck... followed by a police escort.

Before they said their good-bye, the odd couple mentioned, "Fritz would like you to call him at the Mayfair Hotel, which is located close to the city central district and to Tivoli Garden. He said he would like to talk to you before you leave Copenhagen."

"Thanks, I'll call as soon as Nils and I check into a hotel." Seth volunteered.

The man asked, "What hotel is that?"

Seth was quick to respond, "We have reservations at the Mayfair Hotel, also."

"And when are you flying back to the States?" The woman asked.

"My flight leaves the Copenhagen Airport at ten thirty tomorrow morning and Nils is going to hop a short flight to Stockholm at noon tomorrow." Seth informed.

The four shook hands and departed in different directions.

Chapter Eighteen

It was early evening when Seth and Nils checked into the Mayfair Hotel, and the sun was still high in the sky, thanks to the summer solstice in Sweden. The room was sufficient for their needs and both flopped down on a twin bed expressing a relaxed feeling they had not felt in many days. Seth lingered on the bed resting for a short time and Nils fell asleep. The burden of stress had left their mind and body and they were both experiencing the aftermath of a feeling of calmness.

With the safety for the blueprints resolved, Seth's happiness was short lived. Now, looming in his mind is the memory of the intense argument he had with Rachel. He grabbed the telephone and quickly placed a call to his dad.

"Dad, it's me! I'm in Copenhagen." Seth spoke with an urgent need to continue when his dad interrupted.

"Son, I'm glad to hear from you. I hope you are enjoying yourself."

"Well, I have a long story to tell you about blueprints, posters, corporate pirates, the police, Captain Oscarson, and..." Seth was interrupted again.

BillyJoe quipped, "You sure do know how to have exciting trips to various countries in the world. I'll be anxious to hear your story when you come home."

In a very low serious voice, Seth asked, "Dad, have you heard from Rachel?"

"Yes, she called this morning, thinking you would be home today. I told her you were scheduled to fly home tomorrow. Is that right?" BillyJoe asked.

"Yes, I'll be home tomorrow night. I'll take a taxi so you won't have to meet me at the airport." With a worried thought, Seth asked, "Did Rachel say anything?"

"No, she said she would call you later." BillyJoe nonchalantly repeated.

With a sad good-bye, Seth hung up.

Nils woke up, yawned, and asked for the phone to call his office. "Hi, Pete, I thought you would still be in the office. Did I miss anything today?"

"Not much, but we wondered where you were." Pete informed.

"These last few days have been right out of a mystery novel... and do I have a story to tell you! I'll be in the office tomorrow late afternoon. See ya!"

The short rest rejuvenated the two men; and after the stressful, exciting previous days, they were both ready to enjoy the sights and sounds of Copenhagen. Seth rummaged through his luggage for clean clothes after placing the bubble-wrapped package on the nightstand and was ready to call Fritz.

"Hi! It's Seth. Nils and I are right down the hall from your room and we are ready to get something to eat and to see a little bit of Copenhagen."

"Karl and I are ready. We've been waiting for your call. We'll knock on your door in a minute."

The four men thoroughly enjoyed themselves... with no discussion pertaining to the previous few hectic days and nights. Conversation over dinner at the Copenhagen Corner restaurant was relaxing, while Fritz and Karl carefully expounded in detail the excitement of building the Oresund Bridge. They both spoke with pride of being involved in the planning stage of this phenomenal project... a bridge, an artificial island and a tunnel.

Fritz apologized, again, to Seth and Nils for getting them involved, and quickly added, "Just think of the story you will be able to tell your children that you helped to make it all possible."

Seth and Nils looked at one another realizing Fritz is right. They both beamed with the thought and ordered another round of Absolute Vodka martinis so they could toast their good luck.

Walking to Tivoli Garden was another highlight of the evening where they were able to enjoy the musical group *Slick Sound of Tomorrow... from Sweden* on stage with the four posters beautifully displayed bringing closure to a dangerously twisted ordeal. The band members saw the four men standing close to the stage and played a special song for them. After enjoying the music and carnival atmosphere of Tivoli Garden in grandiose style, Fritz and Karl had to take Seth and Nils to a few of the night hot spots in Copenhagen.

It was early in the morning when the four men returned to the hotel. Fritz called to Seth as he was about to enter his room, "Wait a minute, I think you may need this."

Nils stammered in lilting sarcasm, "That bag looks familiar!"

Seth looked at the large blue duffel bag and with a broad grin said, "Thanks, Fritz, you're right."

The four men said their good-byes, promising to keep in touch.

———

It was another short night's sleep as the four celebrated their successful adventure into the wee hours of the morning. But for the first time in several days, Seth was happy to get up early... he was going home. Nils was difficult to awake, but when Seth promised he would buy his breakfast, he rolled out of bed, dressed quickly, packed his suitcase and was out the door before Seth. As they walked the hotel hallway, they could smell the marvelous aroma from the breakfast buffet coming from the restaurant. They enjoyed the Swedish pancakes; Danish cheese, sausage, fruit, coffee and rolls and ate until they felt their ebbing strength was fortified for a day of travel.

Conversation in the taxi during the drive to the airport was constant with both men talking about their desire to go home and return to a normal life... which previously they considered rather mundane, but now that lifestyle is appealing. Seth mostly spoke about his love for Rachel and his desire to make amends for words bitterly spoken.

After listening to Seth's soliloquy on marriage Nils asked, "If married life is so great, how come you have been living in pain these last few days? You're not setting a good example for me. I'm giving second thoughts to proposing to my girl."

In a philosophical mood and with tongue in cheek, Seth wisely quoted from Confucius, "Marriage is like everything else: when it's good, it's great! When it's bad, it's awful!"

"And that's your word of wisdom?" Nils became frustrated with the silly answer and retaliated with, "Yeah, like Confucius would have said that."

Both men started to laugh and, once again, Seth wisely said, "Well... he could have."

The airport terminal was crowded with passengers rushing in all directions to find the right gate for their departure. The floor monitor for flight schedules indicated the international terminal for Seth was at the far end of the building and the local flight for Nils was at the other end.

Seth couldn't pass up the opportunity to say one more time, "So long, curly top!"

Nils shook his head in disbelief and reminded Seth, "Don't lose the duffel bag with the damn vase!"

The two exchanged the secret fraternal handshake remembered from college days; and with broad smiles affirming lasting friendship and with a flip of the hand, both turned to walk the long concourse to their gate.

They were surprised to see the odd couple standing close to the wall, smiling and waving a friendly good-bye.

Part II

Chapter Nineteen

Time weighed heavily on Rachel's heart as if she were living in limbo in a state of uncertainty. It had been only one week since she had last seen Seth, but it may just as well have been an eternity. Heartache and pain had consumed her to a point of being lethargic with no driven compass of life directing her spirit. She believed that by running away from her problem, she could seek solace with the children in the orphanage and her father on the Island of Lantau in China. She tried to show an expression of cheerfulness with the children, but she no longer had the exuberant personality, which they remembered. Only a few years ago, she was their Pied Piper of Hamelin, who told fairytales of beautiful people in far away, mystical lands. Rachel was their angel who helped to fill daytime hours with happiness that allowed them to escape from frightening memories, which haunted nighttime dreams.

General Erik von Horstmann, Rachel's father, reprimanded himself for being selfish, because he was extremely happy Rachel had returned to China. They had worked together building the orphanage on Lantau, which created a tight bond between the two. Before his wife died, he considered the family as a tight threesome, when they survived Hitler's Germany during World War II by escaping to the neutral island of Macau. As he would explain: "Wartime is a brutal teacher for daily survival and the three of us learned to depend on one another." The strength of their love had been tested many times for failure by threats of military and political oppression, but instead their capacity for endurance blossomed to create a home environment filled with precious happiness.

After Rachel left Lantau to return to the States to inherit the Ramsey plantation and to marry Seth, the General's life drastically changed. His home was no longer filled with happiness. With his wife and daughter gone, he was no longer part of a threesome, he was all alone. He had managed to fill the daylight hours working as head of the intelligence office in the Orient... a position demanding his full attention in curbing the rapid expansion of drug trafficking and gold smuggling in Hong Kong and Macau. He did not realize the depth of loneliness in his personal life until Rachel had returned.

Although Rachel did not divulge the reason for her sudden visit, the General surmised it had something to do with Seth. He could hear her soft muffled cries coming from the bedroom at night, and the red puffiness around her eyes in the morning betrayed her attempt to look cheerful. He hoped Rachel would want to take him into her confidence so they could possibly resolve the problem together... just like they used to do years ago. He tried to be both father and mother, but he always realized there were certain questions which arise in a young woman's life when she needs her mother.

The General sat quietly at the breakfast table drinking the last cup of coffee when Rachel entered the kitchen. He flashed a big smile and cheerfully called, "Good morning! How does it feel to sleep in your old bed, again?"

Rachel sadly answered, "Oh, it's okay," and remained quiet as if she were deep into her own thoughts.

Her father waited for her to breach the silence; but with no response, he finally posed the question, "Rachel, it's easy to see you have not been happy these past few days, and I'm here to help you if I can? Something very serious must have happened that has forced you to leave Seth." He put his arm around her in a consoling, loving way and suggested, "Maybe, you will feel better if you talk about it." And he guided her into the parlor where they could sit more comfortably.

Rachel started to sob causing her voice to crack while stuttering to speak, "We had a terrible argument... and it's all my fault!"

The General could not believe what was being told to him and quietly said, "Rachel, don't say that."

"It's true! I never should have agreed to live in that big house on the plantation. For centuries it has been a curse to all women who have lived there. My grandmother gave birth to a bad seed in that house... and the bad seed was my real father." She cried uncontrollably and continued, "You remember the story Seth's father, BillyJoe, told us about the dangerously vicious pranks he would play on people and how mean he was to my real mother." Rachel stopped to think, "That's why my mother moved to Paris... to get away from the house and all the evil omens, which thrive on women's lives. Even BillyJoe's wife left the plantation after a few years, as she, too, was miserable living there."

The General did not interrupt with idle questions as he wanted to let Rachel explain at her own pace the circumstances which necessitated her coming to Lantau.

"Father, I had a miscarriage... I lost my baby and I know it has something to do with that horrible house." And with a frightening thought she cried, "Maybe, I would have given birth to a bad seed."

"Rachel, honey, I didn't know you were expecting a baby."

"I was going to surprise you, but I wasn't even ten weeks pregnant." Rachel lamented, "Seth and I were thrilled we were going to have a baby."

For the first time since Rachel arrived, her eyes had a slight sparkle and then in a solemn tone, she continued, "I can't go back to that house."

The General wanted Rachel to disclose the reason for the argument between her and Seth, but she said nothing more and he did not ask. In her own quiet way, Rachel simply mentioned, "He is suppose to call me tomorrow when he returns from Sweden."

Chapter Twenty

The long flight across the ocean provided Seth with ample time to wallow in a depressive state of mind. The plane cruised high in the sky at twenty-seven thousand feet with large fluffy white clouds floating in their clear domain. In contrast below, the deep blue Atlantic Ocean completed a picture of peaceful serenity. Seth closed his eyes while resting his head against the back of the seat, realizing this was his first opportunity to relax without worrying about blueprints and corporate pirates. He held a glass in his hand hoping the wine would dull his senses a little to obliterate the tortured thoughts regarding his marriage, but he knew it would take more than one glass for that to be accomplished. It had been a long arduous six days, which included deprivation of sleep… and spiked with only a few happy interludes. His brain was frazzled with too many serious thoughts and his spirit had reached its lowest level. He decided to sleep on the plane, hoping to revitalize his energy.

———

It was early evening when the taxi arrived at the plantation. BillyJoe was sitting on the veranda waiting to welcome Seth with open arms. After a fast embrace, BillyJoe carried the one piece of luggage and Seth carried the large blue duffel bag to the house.

BillyJoe quizzically asked, "What's in the duffel bag?"

With a slight smile, Seth replied, "It's a large crystal vase from Christinehof castle in Sweden."

"What? That must be for Rachel!" BillyJoe responded.

"Yes, and if it could talk, it would have quite a story to tell."

BillyJoe was quick to ask, "I want to hear all about it."

After Seth freshened up and grabbed a bite to eat from the kitchen, the two men sat in the swing on the veranda and talked until the early hours of the morning. Seth spoke with alacrity... thoroughly giving a running commentary of every dangerous event. When he mentioned the blueprints were for the construction of a bridge connecting Sweden and Denmark, BillyJoe's eyes widened with curiosity. It had been years since Seth had seen him get so excited, but then he remembered his dad graduated with a civil engineering degree and his heart's desire was to travel the world building beautiful bridges. BillyJoe fired one question after another wanting to know everything about the engineering design of the project.

Seth smiled at his dad's enthusiasm and declared, "Dad... I just looked at the blueprints. I didn't study them. You have too many questions I can't answer." The two men sat for awhile with nothing being said. BillyJoe was consumed with thoughts, where he could vicariously live the engineers' dreams of building this bridge. He was amazed with the magnitude of the design.

Seth was concerned for his happiness and wondered if he regretted not following his heart's desire when he was a young man. He glanced at his dad, who was in his own little dream world, and wondered if he ever felt shackled to the plantation. Seth rested his arm on the back of the swing as they continued to rock, slowly.

BillyJoe looked at his watch and quietly mentioned, "I think we should get some sleep."

———

BillyJoe was preparing Seth's favorite breakfast of egg omelet and bacon, when he entered the kitchen and walked to the stove to put his arm around his dad's shoulder. He bent low over the skillet, smelled the marvelous aroma, and with a broad smile said, "Dad, this is like old times."

With a nostalgic thought, BillyJoe murmured, "Sometimes, I wish we could turn time back."

Seth did not respond, but advised, "I called the office this morning to ask my boss if I could take some vacation time. He was a little reluctant at first because news of corporate pirates' trying to seize certain unpatented blueprints of the Oresund Bridge project had already spread throughout the industry and he is anxious to hear all about the incident." Seth nonchalantly mentioned, "I made up a good convincing story about a family matter that had to be resolved and he finally agreed I could take a week."

BillyJoe asked, "Are you going to China to see Rachel?"

"Yes. Then I called Rachel to give her my flight schedule. I'm flying this afternoon on a flight to San Francisco and then non-stop to Hong Kong."

BillyJoe was disappointed as he had hoped to spend a day or two with him on a one-on-one basis... once again reinforcing a camaraderie the two had established when Seth was a young man. He looked longingly at the kitchen cabinet where he used to keep the bottle of bourbon. After several years of sobriety, he still has a strong craving for just one more shot.

Seth savored every bite of food thinking: *Home cooking is still the best,* but his thoughts dwelled on the short phone call with Rachel. There was no conversation and no words of encouragement to relieve his stress. After he relayed the flight schedule, Rachel ended the call, "Okay... thank you."

Seth thought: *I've had business calls that have lasted longer.*

"Dad, when Rachel called yesterday, thinking I was back in the States, did she say anything or seem upset?" Seth urged.

"Not really," BillyJoe quietly answered, "but she cried a lot before she left for Hong Kong."

The two men sat in the kitchen discussing the growth and prosperity the plantation had gleaned over the past two years. The fields yielded copious crops of tobacco and the commodities market had flourished to greater heights. The company's tobacco warehouses in Le Havre, Athens and Macau were all reporting financial statements indicating a good fiscal year. BillyJoe was quick to praise the office staff in the foreign countries, as well as his loyal staff on the plantation.

They reminisced about Rachel's generosity after she returned from China to inherit the plantation when she relinquished complete ownership by splitting the plantation and business fifty-fifty with BillyJoe... and the whole operation expanded to a grandiose scale. She rewarded BillyJoe for the past generations of hard work, loyalty and devotion his family had shown the Ramsey family.

BillyJoe remarked, "I think my grandfather would be proud."

Seth quickly added, "Dad, you had a lot to do with the prosperity and growth of this plantation and I know he would be very proud of you!"

"Son, when you go home to pack clean clothes for your trip, I'd like you to take a look around the mansion. Rachel hired a couple of new servants before she left and I want to be certain everything is in order and that your private rooms are closed. We are expecting a rather large group of students from the university to tour the antebellum mansion this afternoon. The professor said the students are studying the civil war period and this plantation still has a fine historical reputation... and tourists still talk about the ghost that lives in the mansion."

Seth chuckled, "Dad, that's the best part of the whole tour... and, of course, the wine cellar."

The mention of the wine cellar conjured up old bad memories for BillyJoe and he really wished he had a shot of bourbon.

BillyJoe advised, "I have an important staff meeting this morning so I guess I'll say good-bye, now." With a fatherly hug the two men left the kitchen. BillyJoe turned to call, "Have a safe trip to China."

Chapter Twenty-One

It was late evening when Seth checked into the hotel in city central Hong Kong. After sitting on a plane for many hours, his knees were stiff, his back hurt and he thought it would be a good idea to walk the streets for some much needed exercise. Busses, automobiles and a few rickshaws rumbled down the busy streets with pedestrians pushing their way through the traveled sidewalks. The cacophonous sounds brought a rush of memories, which carried him back to his first visit to Hong Kong when he was searching for Rachel.

The fresh air was invigorating, but he had forgotten the pungent odors coming from all directions: open food markets displaying oriental cuisine of bags of cuttle-fish, pork, chicken, ducks, cat and dog meat, dried rats and much more; and Victoria Harbor, facetiously called Fragrant Harbor for all the discarded garbage, waste and whatever personal effects people no longer need. Hanging red lanterns helped to brighten the colorfully decorated store fronts, restaurants and tea salons, which completed a scenario of commercial activity.

At the end of one long street, he thought he recognized an old friend standing beside a rickshaw with a small covered top, which was supported by long bamboo poles and two wheels attached to a bicycle... and that had to be Chang. Seth continued vigorously pushing his way through the pedestrians, which reminded him of salmon swimming upstream. "Chang! Chang! What a surprise!" He called with a loud voice unable to control his excitement.

The big grin expressed their happiness and with a friendly punch on Chang's arm, Seth asked, "What are you doing in Hong Kong? I thought you were afraid to leave Japan to come home because you didn't want to take a boat and you were afraid to fly." Before Chang could answer, Seth remembered, "Did you consult a feng shui master?"

Chang rolled his eyes, cupped his hands around his head moving it from side-to-side, moaning, "Oh, that very, very, very long story."

Seth cracked up with laughter looking at Chang's pitiful expression and volunteered, "I also have a very long story to tell about a crystal vase I bought in Sweden."

The two remained quiet, deep in their own thoughts. Finally, Seth asked, "Chang, let's get a bite to eat where we can talk. I'll buy."

With a big grin, "You still same good friend. I no eat all day. Business bad. Tourists not come to Hong Kong, now."

Seth hopped into the rickshaw remembering the poverty in China and the Spartan life Chang lives.

The two sat and talked until the restaurant closed; and once again, they said good-bye not knowing if they would ever meet again.

The early morning sun cast a bright ray of light through the one window in Seth's hotel room. He rubbed his eyes vigorously trying to adjust his vision to the brightness not wanting to be awake. He wondered if he ever really fell asleep as his mind churned all night with disturbing ambivalent thoughts not knowing what to expect when he sees Rachel: Yes, he desperately wants to see her; but No, he is worried she may not want to return to the States.

It was after a hearty breakfast in the hotel dining room Seth started to feel like a human being. With suitcase in hand, he left the hotel bracing for the long walk to catch the Star Ferry to Lantau. He thought: *At least I don't have to carry the damn duffel bag.* Seth was surprised to see Chang standing beside his rickshaw in front of the hotel.

"Chang, what are you doing here. I thought we said our good-byes last night!"

"I no like way you look and act last night when we talk. You in deep fog."

Seth started to laugh.

And Chang continued, "I fraid you get lost on way to ferryboat." Chang reprimanded.

Seth shook his head with a silly grin, "Okay. Give me a ride."

The two men bantered back and forth enjoying one another's jargon of Chang's outlandish Pidgin English and Seth imitating Chang in a teasing manner, as the rickshaw rumbled down the road to the Star Ferry.

Chang was reminded of a time several years ago when they said good-bye, and repeated the same sentiment, "If feng shui agree, I like our paths to cross again some day."

With one last embrace Seth said, "I would like that."

———

The short ride on the ferryboat across the Pearl River Estuary to Lantau was a rough ride. He was immediately reminded of the trip aboard the *Ladybug* when crossing the Oresund Strait from Malmo to Copenhagen during the aftermath of the storm a few days ago. He relished the idea of having something else consuming his attention, if only for a short time. The burden of worrying about Rachel for the past week had destroyed his light-hearted temperament. In fact, Seth felt like a physical wreck and in no condition to face Rachel. His body was stiff and ached from sitting for so many hours on the plane; his mental disposition was stressed; and with no sleep he could empathize with a silly thought: *I feel like the bear that couldn't sleep.*

Chapter Twenty-Two

It was mid-morning when Seth arrived at the military compound, which also housed the children's orphanage on Lantau. He was surprised to see so many children playing, while his eyes quickly scanned the playground looking for Rachel.

Rachel saw Seth at the same time and they both were caught in a time lapse. Neither one moved for a few minutes with their eyes transfixed on each other obliterating everyone and anything else.

Seth was startled when he felt a friendly slap on the back.

"Seth, how good to see you!" The general cheerfully called.

Seth shook his head to relieve the mental trance and quickly replied, "General Von, it's great to see you, again."

"I didn't expect to see you until this afternoon. I thought after the long flight you would want to sleep late." The general offered.

"Well, I'm very anxious to talk to Rachel and I really couldn't sleep, anyway." Seth soulfully murmured.

The general volunteered, "Rachel hasn't told me anything, but she cries all the time." The general looked across the playground and saw Rachel walking toward them. "Here she comes; I think I'll leave you two alone." And he strolled away.

Rachel stopped within a foot of Seth. She was so happy to see him forgetting she was mad at him… and she started to cry. Seth did not have a plan as to what he was going to say or do, but his gentle, loving instincts reacted to sooth Rachel's sadness. With a strong gentle touch, he pulled her into his arms, holding her tightly. Rachel closed her eyes when the romantic spell was broken. Some of the little children noticed Rachel was crying and rushed across the playground to see if she were hurt. She slowly pulled away from Seth explaining to the children she had something in her eye, which was causing it to tear, and told a story consoling the children's concern.

The two looked at one another, but said nothing and slowly walked to the house where they could be alone.

Rachel stomped her foot in anger forcefully speaking, "I didn't want to cry, because I'm mad at you. How could you tell me to forget what happened and move on!" She cried uncontrollably and continued, "You don't forget a miscarriage! I think your exact words were, 'Forget it… let it go.'" She stomped her foot again emphasizing, "It's NOT an IT; it's a BABY!"

Seth listened attentively with compassion consuming a heavy heart. He did not realize at the time his words would be misconstrued to be cruel and harsh. His body ached to hold her tightly in an embrace and he kissed her gently in a soothing manner, whispering, "Sweetheart, I love you now and will forever. You are the love of my life and I will never do anything or say anything that may hurt you." Seth choked with emotion and whispered, "I've thought a lot about us this past week. I have been miserable worrying if you even would want to see me. I'm sorry I wasn't more sympathetic and I guess I expressed my thoughts in a cruel way."

Rachel raised her head from his shoulder and looked at Seth with eyes filled with passion. She felt weak in his strong arms, experiencing a ripple of emotions through her body… and she responded to his sweet lingering kiss. The two kissed many times, enjoying the closeness of their bodies and confessing their love will last through eternity, which relieved any anger or tension that had existed.

"Seth," Rachel murmured, "There is no way I can return to the plantation and live in that house. Some people believe it is haunted… with my grandfather, old man Ramsey, walking the halls. I believe there are evil forces that attack women who live there; and I don't want to be the next victim."

Seth knew she was thinking about the Chinese philosophy of feng shui where the earth's energy of wind and water can either provide livelihood and fortune or hardship and misfortune. Her years growing up in China enforced her knowledge of this ancient art and science and she believes there most be a balance of energies... and the mansion on the plantation definitely does not have good Chi, or energy. Seth remained quiet while Rachel continued.

"I know there is much work to be done at the orphanage. Missionaries are coming from small villages seeking sanction from Communist China. We are in the process of constructing apartment buildings for them and their families. We have preachers, teachers and workers devoting their time and energy to work with the children. They all have sad stories to tell about living in mainland China; but after a short time here at the orphanage, a happy environment has been created."

Both were distracted by a noise coming from the kitchen. "Is anyone hungry?" General Von loudly called.

Seth was quick to answer as he did not want to hear Rachel talk about the necessity for her to remain in China, "Yes, I am!"

They joined General Von in the kitchen to eat a light lunch and the three sat and talked for quite awhile.

Seth wanted to plead his case for Rachel to return to the States and suggested, "Rachel, we don't have to live on the plantation. We can live wherever you want. We could build a house closer to town and I could design it to accommodate a daycare center for little children...if you want or feel the need for a project. You certainly have a lot of experience in that area. You could even contact a feng shui master to help me with the design that will provide all good energy." And in a low voice, he mumbled, "Or whatever."

Rachel looked at her father with eyes that glistened showing she approved.

General Von suggested, "Rachel that sounds like a very good idea. With the political unrest in China right now, I think it would be better if you would live in the States. The orphanage has plenty of teachers to provide a good education for the children and a safe environment. I think you should return with Seth... and I know you love him." The general choked with emotion as he hated to see his little girl leave again, but he knew life would be better for her in the States with her husband.

With a wink of his eye at General Von, Seth grabbed Rachel's hand and suggested, "Let's take a walk."

The two lovers took a long walk outside the military compound holding hands and making plans to return to the States. Rachel was already figuring how many bedrooms she wanted in their new house, which would provide rooms for their children. She had not been this happy since the day she and Seth were married. Her complexion literally glowed with a warm color of happiness.

Seth reached in his coat for a small box, which he has had in the pocket for over a week. He stopped on the path, pulled Rachel to him and kissed her.

Rachel questioned, "What's in the box?"

"It's for you. Open it." Seth felt he could burst with happiness.

"Oh, how beautiful! It's a Rolex watch, which I have always wanted. I love it!" Rachel threw her arms around Seth and kissed him.

"Now, you will always know when it is ten o'clock. You will have no excuse not to think of me." Seth flashed a broad smile. "Oh, I have something else for you, too."

"What is it?" Rachel was excited to ask.

"I'll give it to you when we get home." Seth answered.

"Can you give me a hint or tell me what it is?" She coyly asked.

Seth held her tightly and slowly uttered with his lips partly closed, "Well, it's rather large and I brought it home in a blue duffel bag."

"Now, I am curious."

"And it comes with a very long story."

Epilogue

My story begins circa 1958 when the idea to connect Malmo, Sweden with Copenhagen, Denmark was only a vision in the minds of creative architectural engineers. It was first proposed in 1872, but nationalistic objections and most recently environmental concerns were hurdles that had to be resolved by both countries. The idea was actively conceived in 1991 when the governments of Demark and Sweden agreed to undertake this massive project, which crosses the Oresund Strait for a distance of more than ten miles. It is the longest combined road and rail bridge in Europe, consisting of two railroad tracks beneath a four-lane highway. The bridge ends in the middle of the Strait between the two countries where an artificial island was made and belongs to Denmark. It is unpopulated and is maintained as a natural reserve. By necessity, the tunnel was built to accommodate airplanes' flying in and out of Copenhagen airport, which is in close proximity to the construction site. An undersea tunnel completed the causeway linking the two countries and is the largest immersed tunnel in the world.

The design demanded accuracy and precision with many new challenges to be considered to ensure the support construction did not move more than the allotted amount for safety. Laws mandating environmental requirements were strictly considered; such as, noise, vibrations, historical buildings, neighborhoods and ground water level to mention a few. Emergency equipment and communications were installed along escape routes along the length of the link… both in the tunnel and on the bridge.

Construction began in 1995 and was finished three months ahead of schedule in August 1999. Crown Prince Frederik of Denmark and Crown Princess Victoria of Sweden met midway to celebrate its completion. It was officially inaugurated July 1, 2000 with Queen Margrethe II of Denmark and King Carl XVI Gustaf of Sweden presiding at the ceremony. It opened for traffic later that day.

Other books by Jeannine Dahlberg

****

Featuring Seth Coleman and Rachel Ramsey Coleman

Riding the Tail of the Dragon

Candle in the Window

also

A murder mystery

Evil Web of Deceit

About the Author

Jeannine Dahlberg, a native of Missouri, can trace her heritage to mid-seventeenth century Sweden and writing this historic-fiction story became an emotional journey through time where more than a few sidebars to the plot are factual. This novel completes a trilogy to her first two novels, *Riding the Tail of the Dragon* and *Candle in the Window.*

She combines her experience as a writer and her knowledge of foreign travel to tell a story with passion. She lives in St. Louis, Missouri.

LaVergne, TN USA
21 March 2010
176655LV00004B/2/P